CAROLE MORTIMER

perfect partner

Harlequin Books

TORONTO • NEW YORK • LOS ANGELES • LONDON
AMSTERDAM • PARIS • SYDNEY • HAMBURG
STOCKHOLM • ATHENS • TOKYO • MILAN

For
Sheba, Samson and Tabitha

Harlequin Presents first edition February 1983
ISBN 0-373-10571-1

Original hardcover edition published in 1982
by Mills & Boon Limited

CHAPTER ONE

MELANIE was looking her usual beautiful self as she personally opened the door to Juliet. 'Darling!' she moved to kiss her affectionately on the cheek. 'I'm so glad you could come,' she beamed.

Juliet removed her wrap and handed it to the waiting maid. 'You knew I would,' she said dryly. 'But this is positively the last dinner party of yours I come to this month. You know I often work in the evenings. Do you realise this is the fourth time I've been here in as many weeks?'

Her friend gave her an endearing smile, looping her arm through hers to take her through to the lounge. 'It doesn't hurt you to socialise now and again,' she chided.

'I'm too busy.' In fact she had had to rush over here this evening, working almost to the last minute. She hated the interruptions of Melanie's constant dinner parties into her life, but the two of them had been friends since schooldays, something Melanie took advantage of. Melanie had since married Michael Dickson, a publisher, but the girls remained good friends.

She just wished Melanie wouldn't include her in these dinner parties. She didn't enjoy them, and the person picked out as her partner usually managed to bore her to tears.

'You're always too busy, Juliet.' Melanie wasn't in the least concerned about interrupting her work. ' "All work and no play makes Jill a dull girl",' she quoted.

Juliet laughed tolerantly. 'I think you altered that slightly, but the meaning came through.'

'I didn't mean you're dull,' her friend instantly denied.

Juliet smiled, beginning to relax. 'I hope not! Just as I hope tonight's dinner partner is an improvement on last time. The judge you landed me with last week talked of nothing but bringing back the birch. Personally, I thought he was a bit kinky. I know I couldn't wait to get away from him,' she remembered with a shudder.

Melanie smiled. 'You're going to love tonight's partner. And be nice to him, Michael wants him buttered up a little.'

'But who——'

The maid came quietly into the room, attracting Melanie's attention. 'Mr Laurence is here, madam.'

'Thank you, Cindy.' Melanie gave an apologetic look in Juliet's direction. 'We'll talk again later,' she promised. 'Everyone should start to arrive now.'

'Where's Michael?' Juliet asked.

'He's been delayed, some meeting or other,' Melanie grimaced. 'But he promised to be home in time for dinner.'

Juliet knew most of the people who arrived for the dinner party, and chatted amiably with them as she drank her cocktail. Melanie was called out to answer the telephone a short time later, and was frowning when she came back into the room.

Juliet joined her. 'Anything wrong?' she asked softly.

Melanie sighed. 'It's so annoying—Duncan Evans can't make it, he has 'flu or something. It means we'll be thirteen sitting down for dinner.'

Knowing how superstitious her friend was Juliet now understood her distress. 'I have the ideal solution to that, Melanie,' she told her with a smile. 'I'll leave, and then you'll be twelve.'

'You'll do no such thing!' Melanie caught hold of Juliet's arm. 'I'll call Michael and see if he can find someone to bring home with him. Duncan was to be your partner, by the way,' and she hurried out of the room to call her husband.

Juliet vaguely knew of Duncan Evans. He was the editor of a popular women's magazine, and he often serialised the books that Michael published in that magazine. For once it seemed Melanie had chosen someone she would have enjoyed meeting, so it was a pity he had cancelled. Maybe he simply hadn't shared her interest in the meeting, after all she was just Juliet Chase, a school friend of Melanie's.

Melanie looked happier when she came back this time. 'Michael was just leaving, and he was bringing someone with him anyway, so he can take Duncan's place. Thank goodness for that!'

Juliet groaned. 'Who have you foisted on me now? I'd much rather bring my own dinner companion.'

'It's much more fun this way——'

'For whom?' she derided.

'For everyone. Anyway, I'm sure you'll like the man Michael's bringing home, he said he's very presentable.'

'But *who* is he?' Juliet demanded before Melanie had the chance to rush off once again. She never seemed to stand still for more than two minutes at a time!

'I don't know,' Melanie replied vaguely. 'Michael didn't say, and I didn't think to ask. I was just so relieved he could bring someone. I suppose he's just someone who was at this business meeting,' she dismissed.

Juliet silently fumed as her friend disappeared once again. This behaviour was so typical of Melanie. Even at school the other girl had got her into situations she would rather not be in, had almost got them both expelled at one time. This man she had given her as a dinner partner could be a bore or a complete lecher, and Melanie wouldn't give a damn as long as he made up the numbers.

Juliet had a couple of male friends of her own, either one of which she would rather have brought with her.

She wasn't exactly unattractive—on the contrary, Ben and Stephen had individually assured her.

Her hair was deep auburn, shoulder-length, feathered either side of her face. Her eyes were a deep sherry colour, surrounded by thick dark lashes, a light sprinkling of freckles across her small straight nose, her mouth slightly curving, her chin small and pointed, angled determinedly.

At twenty-four she was simply enjoying her life. She had Ben and Stephen, enjoyed her work, and most of all she enjoyed her freedom from emotional entanglements. She dated Ben and Stephen on a casual basis, both of them knew about the other, and so far it had worked out just fine.

Melanie and Michael had been married for three years, and were always advocating the cause of marriage, hence these constant invitations to dinner, the different men she met there. Melanie assured her that if she went to enough of them she was sure to eventually meet a man she was attracted to. So far she hadn't found one of them worth a second meeting.

The man who finally entered the lounge with Michael was completely different from anyone else Melanie had ever introduced to her. He was younger than most of them, for one thing, late thirties, possibly early forties, with thick dark hair tinged with grey at the temples, giving him a distinguished air. His face was strong and a little harsh, the dark blue eyes now narrowed on the other occupants of the room, his nose long and straight, a mocking twist to the firmness of his mouth, and there was a deep cleft in the squareness of his chin, his jaw was firm. He was very tall, powerfully built like an athlete, and yet he had long artistic-looking hands.

The dark brown suit he wore fitted perfectly across his broad shoulders, tapered to his narrow waist and tautly muscled thighs. He was a handsome devil, ruggedly so, and he seemed aware of his own attraction, if only subconsciously, his self-assurance unmistakable, his expression faintly contemptuous now.

He seemed vaguely familiar, the arrogant angle of that dark head, the determination in the broad shoulders, the mockery in deep blue eyes. Yes, he was very familiar to Juliet, and yet she felt sure she would have remembered that leashed air of excitement, the magnetism that could never be overlooked. No, she had never met this man before, but she did know him. At that moment she just couldn't remember where from.

Michael was introducing him to Melanie now, the other girl blushing prettily as he obviously made some complimentary remark to her. And now Melanie was bringing him over to her.

His gaze was frankly assessing as it passed from the auburn gleam of her hair, down over the figure-hugging black dress, and even further down the length of her long legs to her sandal-clad feet. His gaze finally returned to her face, and Juliet met that gaze unflinchingly, seeing the flicker of interest in his expression.

Even though she was tall herself this man towered over her by several inches, putting him at about six foot two or three, close to the smell of his tangy aftershave pleasant to the senses.

Melanie smiled happily at them both, obviously relieved to at last have all her guests together. 'Juliet, I want you to meet Jake Matthews. Jake, this is my good friend Juliet Chase. Now I'll leave you two to get acquainted while I go and check with Cook about dinner. I do hope it isn't ruined,' and she moved away with a worried frown.

Juliet had stiffened as soon as this man's name was revealed to her. Jake Matthews! No wonder he seemed so familiar to her—he hosted a book review programme once a week on television, and wrote a weekly column in one of the more outspoken newspapers. She should have recognised him, his arrogance was unmistakable, his air of mockery.

She only hoped he didn't talk as caustically as he wrote, or criticise the way he did on television, otherwise she was in for a more unenjoyable evening than usual. This man could ruin a book's sales with just one word of criticism from him, just as he could make it number one on the bestseller list, and she could only wonder at Michael's apparent friendship with such a man. Still, perhaps he considered it better to be friends with one's critics than to have them for an enemy. Michael was an astute enough businessman to have realised that.

'Mr Matthews,' she acknowledged curtly.

'Miss Chase,' he drawled, taking a swallow of the whisky in his glass. 'I hear your dinner partner let you down.'

Sherry-coloured eyes widened with indignation. 'I didn't have one,' she bristled at his tone. 'One of Melanie's guests is ill and can't make it. I'm sorry if you feel you've had me foisted on you, but I can assure you——'

'I didn't say that, Miss Chase,' he cut in softly. 'And I didn't imply it either. As a matter of fact, I was just congratulating myself on my luck.'

Juliet looked startled. He didn't appear to be the sort of man to throw out idle compliments, so she had to assume he meant this one. Her expression was cold, her reason for disliking this man too deep-rooted for it to be charmed out of her by a few meaningless compliments.

'Thank you,' she accepted tightly. 'Your programme is—interesting, Mr Matthews.'

'Thanks. And if I can call you Juliet you can call me Jake.'

The wording of that statement made it impossible for her to refuse. 'Please do.' She looked over to where Melanie was frantically trying to attract her attention. 'I think we're being summoned to eat.'

As she had known, and dreaded, Melanie had seated them next to each other at the table, and Jake Matthews made it very clear he intended taking full advantage of the fact.

He held her chair out for her before lowering his tall frame into the chair next to her. 'So,' he turned to look at her, his closeness curiously intimate, 'how do you fit in among these famous authors, television stars, exclusive barristers, and—My God, a cricket player!' He gave a soft laugh as he looked at the leading player in the English team. 'How do you suppose he got in here?' he mocked.

'He's an old friend of Michael's,' Juliet supplied stiffly.

He quirked one dark eyebrow. 'And you?'

'An old friend of Melanie's. And as you're a famous book critic, *the* most famous book critic, it's obvious how you got in,' she said cattily.

'Do I sense criticism of your own?' he taunted.

She gave him a cool look from eyes that should have been the colour of warm sherry—only there was no warmth to them at all. 'I don't know, do you?'

'I think so,' he said slowly, his expression thoughtful. 'Why is that, Juliet? You don't even know me.'

And she didn't intend to either, self-opinionated, arrogant fool! 'Maybe I just don't agree with some of your opinions. Your remarks can be very cutting at times.'

Jake Matthews shrugged his broad shoulders. 'If the authors can't take it then they shouldn't write. A book is there to be criticised.'

'It's there to be enjoyed, surely,' she disagreed heatedly, two bright spots of angry colour heightening her cheeks.

'If it's good I enjoy it, if it's bad I say so,' he told her in a bored voice.

'I've noticed,' she snapped. 'A couple of months ago

you ripped *Devil's Dare* by Gregory James to pieces. I found it totally spoilt my own enjoyment of it.' And as Gregory James happened to be one of the best-selling thriller writers in the world, and a particular favourite with her, she had found this man's criticism infuriating. 'All the time I was reading the book I kept looking for the loopholes in the plot that you'd outlined in your programme,' she added disgustedly.

'Well, if they hadn't been there you wouldn't have found them. Did you?' he drawled.

'You know I did,' she revealed resentfully.

'Yes,' he acknowledged, as if his point had been proved. '*Devil's Dare* was simply a rip-off. The man's made his name now, and so he thinks he can dish up any old—rubbish to the public, and that they'll buy it. The irony of it is that a lot of people went out and bought the book simply because I criticised it.'

Her mouth twisted. 'What's it like to be disliked so much?'

He smiled, a completely relaxed smile. 'I can assure you that not everyone dislikes me, in fact I have quite a fan-club of my own.'

For his undoubted good looks perhaps, but certainly not for his outspoken views. 'Your criticism of Caroline Miles was a bit unfair too. I've never known Michael to publish a book unless he personally thought it was good. And he hasn't got to be a successful publisher by choosing duds.'

Jake Matthews looked unperturbed. 'I simply said what I thought,' he said tolerantly, obviously not taking this seriously.

'That "Miss Miles should stop trying to relive the memories of her lost youth through her books",' she quoted. 'I think by that you meant to imply that Caroline Miles is a dried-up old spinster who should stick to her knitting!'

Once again he smiled, a charming smile that must

have captured many a female heart. But it didn't even cause Juliet's to flutter! She was immune to men like this, and especially Jake Matthews.

'You understand me well, Juliet,' he drawled. 'That's exactly what I meant.'

'And is she? A dried-up old spinster, I mean?' she asked interestedly.

He gave a soft laugh. 'I have no idea. I've never had the misfortune to meet the lady.'

'Poor woman,' she sympathised. 'Convicted without a trial,' she explained at his questioning look.

'Have you read *Mason's Heritage*?' he asked interestedly, leaning forward, his elbow on the table as he sipped his wine, but continuing to watch her over the rim of the glass.

'Yes,' she snapped.

He nodded, as if suspecting as much. 'Did you like it?'

'Yes,' her voice was taut now. 'And so did a lot of other people.'

'Mm, I heard it had a very good response.' He shrugged. 'Maybe you should be the critic and not me, Juliet.'

'Maybe I should,' she agreed challengingly.

His eyes openly mocked her. 'I'll suggest it to my producer and editor.'

'You do that.' She turned away angrily, eating her meal in furious silence.

Overbearing know-it-all! She couldn't stand people who were as opinionated as this man—and he did it for a living! And Melanie must have known she would rather be anywhere than sitting next to this man. This was positively the last time she came to one of these dinner parties, friend or no friend.

'Besides what I do for a living,' that now familiar lazy drawl interrupted her thoughts, 'what else have I done to offend you?'

Sherry-coloured eyes flashed as she looked up at him. 'Isn't it enough?' she snapped.

'I wouldn't have thought so, no.' His gaze was warm as he made no effort to hide his attraction to her.

'I've invariably found that the job is the man,' she told him haughtily.

'I do other things besides book reviews.'

'Oh yes?' she said uninterestedly.

'Yes,' his eyes had hardened to icy chips, giving her a brief glimpse of the ruthless man beneath the surface charm. 'It just so happens that I enjoy my work.'

'I'm sure you do!'

He sat back. 'Why are you taking this so personally?' he asked easily. 'Do you get upset at every critic's views, or just mine?'

'Yours tend to be more outspoken than most.'

'You don't have to watch the television programme, or read the column in the newspaper,' he pointed out reasonably.

'Oh, but I do,' she smiled coolly. 'I like to see what outrage you're going to come out with next. Your attack on Gregory James was almost personal.'

'And Caroline Miles?'

Her mouth twisted. 'When you know nothing about the woman it can hardly be called personal.'

He looked at her for several minutes, his gaze admiring. 'I'll tell you what, Juliet,' he finally said. 'You write a book and I'll tell everyone what a beautiful woman you are, very independent, intelligent, and prepared to stand up for what you believe to be right.'

Juliet blushed at his description of her. She had believed that, like most men, he would see only the surface attraction and not bother with the intelligent woman inside the body. But Jake Matthews was turning out to be a bit of a surprise altogether. Most people would have accepted her earlier snub, or at least avoided the subject that had caused it, but this man had gone straight back to it.

'Wouldn't that be rather unfair? Besides, I'd probably write a poor story.'

'What work do you do?' he asked interestedly.

'I work for Michael.' She sipped her wine.

Jake smiled. 'Then you're in the right place to get your book published.'

'Have you ever written one?' She couldn't ever remember seeing a book written by this man, but that didn't mean there wasn't one. Besides, if he had any sense he would write under a pseudonym, as the nature of his profession meant his fellow-workers were likely to be over-critical about any book bearing the name Jake Matthews.

'Never,' he laughed softly. 'And I'm never going to. You?'

'I wrote one once,' she revealed slowly.

'What happened to it?'

Juliet shrugged dismissively. 'It's at home somewhere, turned down by a publisher. Perhaps I should let you read it, get your opinion. On second thoughts, maybe I'd better not. The sort of criticism you dish out would break me.'

He gave a husky laugh, a deep attractive sound that caused several of the other women present to turn and look at him. Juliet realised for the first time that she was actually being envied her dining companion, that most of the other women here would gladly take her place.

She looked at Jake Matthews with new eyes, seeing a wealth of experience in the deep cynicism of his face, a knowledge of women in those narrowed blue eyes that hadn't been learnt just by looking at them. This man was at least thirty-five, there would have been many women in his life, could even be one now. He could even be married for all she knew!

'I'd be very gentle on you, Juliet,' he promised softly.

She searched his strong features for some sign of a double meaning, but could find none. But Jake had been flirting with her, she knew that. She hadn't reached her mid-twenties without learning something of men, and Jake Matthews definitely found her attractive. 'What would your wife think of you showing such favouritism?' she asked pointedly.

His mouth quirked with humour, seeing right through her line of questioning. 'I'm not married, Juliet.'

Her eyebrows rose as she couldn't hide her surprise at his single state. 'Have you ever been?'

'No. Have you?'

'No,' she replied tightly.

'I'm sure you've had offers, though,' he taunted.

'Several,' she confirmed stiffly.

'And I've never offered once,' he drawled.

She knew that. If he had offered he would have been accepted. There would be few women who would turn him down. 'You're quite old not to be married,' she said bluntly.

'So are you,' he replied as candidly. 'What are you, twenty-three, twenty-four?'

'Twenty-four. And you, over or under forty?'

'Under,' he grinned. 'I'm thirty-eight. Now that we have the question of married status and age out of the way perhaps we can get to know each other a little better. Do you have any family, Juliet?'

'Just my mother. She lives in Devon. And you?' If he could ask personal questions then so could she!

He shrugged. 'No parents, just a sister. She's married to an American, living in California with her husband and two unruly brats.'

'You don't like children?'

'I didn't say that,' he denied. 'I like them well enough, and probably one day I'll have a couple of my own. I certainly don't intend remaining single for ever. I just haven't found my other half yet.'

Juliet held back her gasp of surprise. 'You really believe that everyone has a perfect partner?'

'Yes,' he nodded, grinning suddenly. 'It's a pity they rarely meet.'

'You're cynical!' Juliet snapped.

'Realistic,' he corrected. 'But I'll marry one day, if only to have children. But they won't become beach-bums,' he added grimly.

'Is that what's happened to your sister's children?'

'Yes. The eldest one has already dropped out of school, the other one will soon follow. It's a damned waste.'

'And you?' Juliet eyed him with amusement. 'Did you dutifully finish your education?' He didn't appear to her to be the sort of man who would welcome the leash of authority, and she doubted he had been any different in his youth.

'No,' he smiled, that devastating smile that even Juliet was finding she wasn't immune to. If anything he looked even more attractive when he smiled, his eyes a deeper blue, crinkled at the corners, his teeth very white against his tanned skin, the cleft in his chin more prominent. 'But then you knew that, didn't you?'

'I guessed,' she smiled back, and then stopped herself. The unaccustomed wine was making her enjoy talking to a man she should despise, in fact she was starting to like him, which wouldn't do at all. 'What did you do instead?' Her tone was more stilted.

'I went to sea for a couple of years. You grow up fast that way.'

'I can imagine,' she grimaced. It was a hard life, and Jake still kept himself very fit by the look of him, very lean and firmly muscled. It wasn't the body of a man who sat behind a desk all day. 'Did you like it?'

'I enjoyed the stops in port—and I didn't have a girl in every one,' he added at her knowing look. 'Just a couple of them,' he grinned. 'Believe me, after several months on board it's nice to have someone to—go home to.' He grimaced. 'I stuck it for a couple of years before hitch-hiking over America. I really liked that. I did any work going to pay my way. Then when I got back to England I got a job as an errand boy on one of the big newspapers. I loved it—the tension, the excitement, the sheer hard work that went into putting out a newspaper every day. It was as if I'd come home.' He shrugged. 'I knew that atmosphere was for me.'

Juliet had been mesmerised by the different emotions flitting across his ruggedly tanned features. That he enjoyed his work was obvious, his expression one of tense excitement as he spoke of it.

'Unfortunately, I can't write,' he added ruefully. 'I tried for a while, but it was no good. But I've always liked reading, anything I could get my hands on, so I was finally taken on as assistant to the book critic of the time. When he retired I was chosen to take his place. The television programme came out of writing the column. A television studio has a similar atmosphere to a newspaper, everyone knowing what their job is, and determined to do it to the best of their ability.'

'Including you,' she recalled dryly.

'Especially me,' he nodded. 'Juliet——'

'Hey, you two,' Melanie appeared behind them, 'everyone else has gone through to the lounge for coffee.'

And they had too. Juliet had been so intent on their conversation, so interested in spite of herself, that she had forgotten everyone else at the table, and she could tell by Jake's almost surprised expression that he had too.

He stood up, pulling back her chair for her. 'Forgive us, Mrs Dickson. I'm afraid Juliet has been too good a listener. I must have been boring her out of her mind.' He gave a smile that said he knew she had been anything but bored.

She smiled at him politely, not denying the statement, watching as the smile died out of his eyes, even if his mouth remained smiling.

'Come into the other room and have some coffee,' Melanie encouraged. 'You can continue talking in there.'

Juliet excused herself as soon as they reached the lounge, escaping thankfully to the bathroom. Jake Matthews was very easy to listen to, was fascinating in fact, and without realising it she had enjoyed being with him, had enjoyed his intelligence and humour.

But she wasn't going to get involved with him. Despite her preconceived dislike of him she knew he wouldn't be as easy to handle as Ben or Stephen either, all of their attempts at a more intimate relationship duly rebuffed by her. It might be old-fashioned in this day and age to reject physical intimacy, but she did so every time. She wasn't a complete innocent, but in the true meaning of the word she was, never having met a man she wanted to be that close to. And Jake Matthews wasn't that man either!

Melanie was waiting outside for her as she left the bathroom, and dragged her into the adjoining bedroom. 'Well?' her blue eyes glowed mischievously. 'What do you think of Jake?'

She wasn't even sure of that herself! 'I hardly know the man,' she evaded.

'He likes you, I can tell.'

'Don't be silly, Melanie.' Juliet vigorously brushed her auburn hair into gleaming waves and re-applied her lipgloss, satisfied with her coolly composed reflection. 'We've just been talking, that's all.' She turned from the mirror, shutting her small evening bag with a snap.

'What about?' her friend asked expectantly.

'Oh, this and that,' she evaded.

Melanie raised one blonde eyebrow; she was the complete opposite of Juliet, being small, bubbly and blonde.

'That?' she queried suggestively.

'Not that,' Juliet sighed. 'Really, Melanie, I've only just met the man! Even you wouldn't discuss sex with a complete stranger.'

'I might, if he looked like Jake.'

'You wouldn't,' she smiled. 'But I really am very angry with you for putting the two of us together,' she sobered. 'You know what I think of him and his sarcasm.'

'Did you tell him?'

'I certainly did.'

'And?'

'And he didn't seem to mind,' she admitted reluctantly.

'Maybe he can take criticism,' Melanie teased.

'I should think he would have to,' Juliet said bitchily. 'He's so often wrong.'

Her friend laughed happily. 'I must go and talk to Michael, he's dying to know how you got on with Jake.'

'Don't bother,' Juliet mouth twisted, 'I'll tell him myself.'

'But what about Jake?' Melanie gasped.

Juliet smiled at the other girl. 'You go and entertain him,' she opened the bedroom door. 'Afer all, he's your guest.'

'But——'

'I'm just going to have a word, in fact a few words,' she amended pointedly, 'with your husband, and then I'm leaving.' She quickly left the room, before Melanie had time to protest any further.

Jake Matthews was talking to one of the other guests, the cricket player he had derided being here, as Juliet made her way over to Michael's side. But Jake seemed to know of her presence in the room, his narrowed gaze following her progress across the room, watching as she talked to Michael. And that blue-eyed gaze could be very unnerving.

'You louse!' she instantly accused Michael.

'Me?' he feigned innocence. At twenty-five he had inherited his father's publishing company, and now, five years later, entirely due to his judgment, Dickson Publishing was one of the few publishers not to be suffering difficulty in this time of high prices and high interest rates. 'What did I do?' he grinned goodnaturedly.

'Not just you,' she scowled. 'Melanie helped. I suppose you both thought it was very amusing. And don't pretend not to know what I'm talking about,' she carried on as he went to speak, 'because I know you both too well for that. The two of you make a good comedy act!'

'Now just calm down, Juliet,' he patted her arm soothingly. 'I'd forgotten you were going to be here tonight. Honestly,' he insisted at her look of outrage.

'You wouldn't know honesty if it sat up and bit you!' she dismissed scathingly.

'Now, Juliet, that's hardly fair——'

'Fair!' she cut in crossly. 'That isn't in your vocabulary either. Really, Michael, you're just asking for trouble having us in the same room together, let alone actually sitting us next to each other.'

He shrugged. 'I didn't notice any fights that end of the table, not physical ones anyway.'

'That's because Juliet is too much of a lady to hit a man in public,' drawled the now familiar voice of Jake Matthews. He looked down at her as he came to stand at her side. 'Melanie tells me that you're leaving, and that you usually get a taxi.' He took a firm hold of her arm. 'I'll take you home, then you can—hit me in private,' he winked at the other man.

Juliet glared up at him resentfully, although some of her anger was directed at Melanie. She usually left her car at home when she came to one of these dinner parties, conscious of the alcohol level, but Melanie didn't have to go and tell Jake Matthews that.

'Let go of my arm,' she ordered. 'Will you let go!' she

repeated as he made no effort to do so. 'If you don't let me go,' she warned softly, 'I'm likely to hit you now, public or no public.'

He studied her mutinous face in silence for several long minutes. 'I believe you would too,' he said slowly.

'She would,' Michael told him dryly. 'Take my advice, Jake, and let her go.'

He made no effort to do so, but looked calmly at Michael. 'If she hits me I'm going to kiss her,' he revealed softly.

'You wouldn't!' Juliet gasped.

Those deep blue eyes were now turned on her. 'Try me,' he challenged softly.

He would do it, she could see that in the steadiness of his gaze, the determination of his jutting jaw. 'Would you please release my arm, Mr Matthews?' she requested tightly, hating the use of his superior strength. Unlike a lot of women nowadays she was quite prepared to admit that in physical strength most men were superior to women, although she didn't believe they were superior in any other way!

'Jake,' he corrected huskily.

'Jake,' she said through gritted teeth, sure that he was bruising her arm.

'Certainly I'll let you go, Juliet.' She was instantly set free. 'Now, are you ready to leave?'

'I'm not going anywhere with you, you——'

'I could still kiss you,' he affably interrupted her angry tirade.

She looked over at the grinning Michael. 'Well, don't just stand there,' she snapped. 'Help me!'

He was looking at the other man with open admiration. 'I've always wanted to do something like that,' he spoke almost in awe. 'But I don't think Melanie would stand for it,' he added ruefully.

'Neither will I!' Juliet exploded. 'Mr Matthews, you——'

'We're leaving, Michael,' Jake once again grasped Juliet's arm. 'Say goodnight to your lovely, and helpful, wife for us.'

The last Juliet saw of Michael was as Jake Matthews bundled her across the room and out of the house. She had never been treated so high-handedly in her life before, and was literally speechless as the passenger door of the Ferrari was opened for her, Jake walking around the back of the car to get in behind the wheel, his presence at once overwhelming.

'Did I bore you that much?' he asked once they had been driving in silence for several minutes.

Juliet blinked dazedly, her lashes long and silky. 'Bore me?' she repeated.

'Mm,' he nodded. 'So much so that you escaped the first opportunity you could.'

'I didn't escape!' Her eyes flashed like a sparkling red wine. 'I was simply talking to Michael. We were at a dinner party, Mr Matthews, it's usual to converse with one's host.'

'You would have come back to me?'

'No, I wouldn't! We didn't go there together, I saw no reason to stay at your side,' she scowled.

'But I saw every reason for staying at yours,' he smiled that infuriating smile. 'I like the way you look, Juliet. And I like your spirit. Will you have dinner with me tomorrow?'

'Certainly not,' she replied irritably. 'You see, I don't like anything about you.'

'Nothing?' he quirked one dark eyebrow questioningly.

'Nothing,' she told him rebelliously.

He slowed the car right down, turning off into a side-road before stopping the car completely. He left the engine running as he turned in his seat to look at her. 'You have the most beautiful eyes I've ever seen,' he said almost incredulously, his hand at her nape pulling her slowly towards him. 'The colour of sherry,' he murmured throatily.

She watched him almost as if in a dream, was conscious of his movements and yet unable to stop him. She knew he was going to kiss her seconds before his mouth claimed hers, knew it and yet didn't fight him. Let him take his kiss, it was easier than fighting him, and she would never see him again after tonight anyway. She waited resignedly, wishing it over.

But the second his lips touched hers she knew this was no ordinary kiss. Jake held her face between his hands as his mouth discovered hers, as his lips probed and parted hers with throbbing urgency, their ragged breathing the only sound in the car, the air between them charged with electricity.

When Jake finally moved back they were both pale, Juliet's eyes, the eyes that had apparently prompted the kiss, wide with bewilderment. She had been kissed by other men, quite a few in fact, and yet her senses still swam from the impact of this one.

'Dinner tomorrow?' he repeated persuasively.

Her hand resting on his chest told her his heart was beating as erratically as her own. 'What time?' she heard herself ask breathlessly.

'Eight-thirty?'

'Fine,' she nodded.

'Juliet . . .' he groaned before his lips once more claimed hers.

It was just like before, that same liquid fire in her veins, that same dizzy feeling, as if she had drunk too much champagne. And yet she had only had a couple of glasses of wine, so it wasn't that. No, it was this man making her feel drunk, with passion.

'No, Jake!' She managed to gain enough strength to wrench away, coming slowly to her senses. 'Please, we're on view here!' She straightened her hair.

Jake still held her, his lips nuzzling her throat. 'Your place or mine?'

'Neither.' She moved completely out of his arms, her voice edged with the shock she couldn't hide. 'You like to work fast, Mr Matthews,' she said tautly.

He shrugged. 'I usually know what I want, and how to get it.'

As he had known exactly how to get her to agree to seeing him tomorrow! She had acted like the besotted fool he had made her feel. 'Not tonight,' she told him coldly.

'Too soon?'

Her blood boiled at his arrogance. 'Much too soon.' It would always be too soon for them! 'My home is the other way,' she pointed to distantly as she realised where they were parked.

'Okay, direct me,' he accepted her refusal resignedly, and turned in his seat to accelerate the car back out into the flow of traffic.

Juliet silently fumed at him as they travelled to her home. Arrogant fool! And she was even more of a fool for letting him affect her in this way.

'Are you going to invite me in for coffee?' he asked once they were parked outside her home.

'Not tonight. I—I'm a little tired,' she feigned weariness.

One of those long artistic hands came out and touched her pale cheek. 'All right, Juliet.' That attractively curved mouth was once more coming her way. 'God, I want you badly,' he told her before kissing her with a savagery designed to take her breath away.

But it didn't. This time she was ready for him, her anger stopping her from responding, the sheer audacity of the man making her furious. He *wanted* her! And no doubt he thought it would be easy to get her into bed with him. He was in for a surprise if he really thought that. She wouldn't be taken unawares again.

He moved back, shrugging at her lack of response. 'As you say, you're tired. So I'll say goodbye until tomorrow.'

Juliet hastily left the intimacy of the car, forcing herself to turn and wave to Jake before he drove off. She had been wrong about him, he was a typical male chauvinistic pig if ever she had met one! And she had met plenty of them in the past, although Jake Matthews came a definite first for chauvinism.

He was the type of man she most despised, after all, the sort of man who didn't think women had a brain, that they were only there to cook and provide sexual pleasure for men. She always liked to be an equal partner in her relationships with men, in fact she insisted on it, and as far as Jake Matthews was concerned she hadn't been allowed to make one decision for herself. She didn't know what sort of women he was usually attracted to, but she certainly wasn't one of those women who were just grateful to be thought worthy of sharing the television personality's bed.

The telephone was ringing when she entered her flat, and she didn't need two guesses who it was. 'Hello, Melanie,' she greeted dryly, sitting down in the chair next to the telephone, knowing from experience how long Melanie's telephone calls usually were.

'Hello.' Her friend wasn't in the least abashed that she had known it was her. 'I just called to see how Jake enjoyed kissing that dried-up old spinster Caroline Miles. He did kiss you, didn't he?' Melanie asked excitedly.

CHAPTER TWO

HEAVENS, yes! She had forgotten all about being Caroline Miles in her anger, had forgotten her pseudonym. What a shock Jake Matthews was going to get when he found out he told that 'dried-up old spinster' that he *wanted* her, badly, and had actually shown her how badly. What a lovely revenge on him, on him and his damned arrogance!

It would be sheer joy to see his face when he was told the truth, in fact it was worth going out with him, putting up with his chauvinism, just for the anticipation of being able to tell him that *she* was Caroline Miles, and that it was her book *Mason's Heritage* that he had called 'romantic rubbish'.

She had watched his programme in stunned disbelief, had read his review with tears in her eyes, hurt by his criticism, and it wasn't until she had finished crying her heart out that anger had taken over. It was then that she had told Melanie and Michael that if she ever had the misfortune to meet the insulting Jake Matthews she would tell him exactly what *she* thought of *him*. Now that she had her chance she would make the most of it, would choose a time when it would have the most effect.

'Juliet?' Melanie interrupted her pleasurable anticipation. 'Juliet, are you still there?'

She had forgotten all about poor Melanie! 'Yes, of course I'm still here,' she hastily assured her.

'Well, did he kiss you? He must have done,' Melanie answered herself. 'Michael said he was being very forceful.'

'Michael also said he wished he dared be that way

with you,' Juliet recalled dryly.

'He never would be,' Melanie said confidently. 'What did Jake think of your being Caroline Miles?'

'He didn't think anything—he doesn't know.'

'You didn't tell him?' her friend gasped her astonishment.

'No. And I would be grateful if you and Michael would refrain from telling him too.'

'Why?' her friend asked suspiciously.

'Because I'm saving that little surprise for a more appropriate time.'

'Appropriate?'

'Yes,' Juliet dismissed impatiently. 'Do you know he actually wanted to go to bed with me?' she revealed indignantly, finding she became angry just at the thought of it. No man had ever pursued her that forcefully on their first meeting before. And she didn't like it. Jake Matthews had known her only long enough to want her body, certainly not long enough to be interested in the person she was. And how that infuriated her! He would probably have expected her to cook his breakfast in the morning too, before he rushed off to his office, never to be seen again.

'I gathered that much from Michael,' Melanie giggled.

'I mean now, tonight.'

'Yes,' her friend acknowledged.

Juliet frowned. 'Aren't you shocked?'

'No. But you are, I can tell. And I always thought you were liberated.'

'Not that liberated!'

'Don't be such a prude, Juliet,' Melanie chided. 'There's nothing wrong in going to bed with a man if it's what you both want. And Jake's certainly too old to go in for the hand-holding, gazing-into-your-eyes relationship. So are you, come to that,' she added thoughtfully.

She hadn't thought she was. Surely love and romance weren't completely dead? No wonder she preferred to write about the past, to imagine herself back in a time when men weren't ashamed to love and protect a woman.

Heavens, what a contradiction she was! She wasn't prepared to relinquish an ounce of her freedom, not careerwise or emotionally, and yet she secretly longed to be swept off her feet, to be cherished, to be made to feel the most important thing in some man's life. One of her ideals would have to go, and she had a feeling, in this day and age, that it would be the latter. One of these days she would probably settle down to marriage quite happily, a marriage where she would be allowed to feel an equal partner but would never know what it was like to be the very pinnacle of one man's existence.

'Don't you think a few hours' acquaintance is rather brief notice of an invitation to bed?' she asked Melanie mockingly.

'Depends on the man,' her friend answered seriously. 'Jake doesn't appear to be the sort to waste time.'

'Well, I think he could have wasted a little more time than he did!' Juliet said waspishly.

'Are you seeing him again?'

'I may be,' she evaded.

'Which means you are,' Melanie said excitedly. 'And Michael and I are to keep quiet about your writing. Don't take Jake for a fool, Juliet, that's all I ask. On the outside he's perfectly charming, but inside there beats a heart of steel. I also happen to know,' she added slowly, 'that there's a certain Patricia Hall in his life at the moment. She's a reporter on the same newspaper he works for.'

No wife, but a girl-friend. 'I'm only having dinner with him, he's perfectly free to keep—Patricia Hall, I think you said? I have no intention of giving up Ben and Stephen on the basis of one date with Jake Matthews.'

'It may develop into more than that. If he'd looked at me the way he looked at you . . .!'

'You wouldn't be here alone now, I suppose,' Juliet teased.

'Juliet! You know Michael was the first and only man I've ever slept with!' Melanie sounded hurt.

'I'll never know how.'

'Well, really!'

Juliet laughed. 'Before you explode I think you should know I was only teasing. It's just that when we were at school you seemed to fall in love every other month.'

'That's a slight exaggeration,' Melanie told her indignantly. 'And I was never truly in love until I met Michael.'

'I'll tell him how loyal you are the next time I see him,' Juliet mocked gently.

'Oh, you're impossible!' Melanie said disgustedly. 'I'll call you on Friday to see how you got on.'

'Not too early,' Juliet taunted. 'You never know, I might not be alone.'

'You should be so lucky!' Melanie gave an angry snort before ringing off.

She really shouldn't tease her friend in that way, but Melanie had always been so easy to tease, pretending a sophistication she just didn't have. And she would try to run her life for her. Even at school she had arranged blind dates for her. Unfortunately this habit had carried on through adulthood.

Juliet changed into serviceable denims and a tee-shirt, then went into her study to finish writing the chapter she had had to leave earlier. She was writing the sequel to *Mason's Heritage*, continuing the story of the Mason family from the late 1800s where she had last left them.

She hated the constant interruptions to her work and found it difficult to get back into the story, liking to choose the moment she broke off from her work, often losing an idea completely if she were forced to leave it for a day or so.

Maybe she should move away from London, away from the interruptions, she certainly had enough money to do that; *Mason's Heritage* was very profitable. But she had lived in London for the last seven years, in the same apartment, and couldn't really see any reason to change.

It was after three by the time she put an end to Chapter Five, and before going through to her bedroom she left the handwritten sheets beside her typewriter to be typed in the morning.

It seemed as if her head had barely touched the pillow, blessed sleep taking over, when the telephone on her bedside table began to ring. The shock of it made her shoot up in bed, a sick feeling washing over her. She snatched up the receiver. 'Yes?' she snapped, a painful thumping starting at the back of her eyes due to lack of sleep.

'Oh, good,' a familiar male voice greeted. 'I'm glad I caught you before you went to the office.'

Office? What office? She blinked to clear the sleep from her brain. 'Who is that?' she demanded crossly.

'Forgotten me already?' the man gave a throaty laugh. 'That isn't very flattering.'

Jake Matthews! She *had* forgotten all about him. 'What time is it?' she groaned, collapsing back against the pillows.

'Almost eight o'clock.'

'Oh, God. . . .' she closed her eyes. No wonder she didn't feel as if she had been to sleep—she hadn't!

'Did I wake you?' the idea suddenly seemed to occur to him.

She sighed. 'Whatever gave you that idea?' she snapped.

Jake gave a throaty chuckle. 'You should be thanking me.'

'I should?'

'Mm, I've stopped you being late for work.'

Work? Goodness, yes, he thought she worked for Michael at Dickson Publishing. 'I wasn't going into the office today. Is there any special reason for your call?' Perhaps he was going to cancel their date for tonight. The way she felt at the moment she could sleep the whole day *and* night away.

'I just wanted to make sure I hadn't dreamt you,' he told her huskily.

'And?'

'I haven't,' he said with satisfaction.

Heavens, this man was a flirt! No doubt she was supposed to feel flattered by this early morning show of attention. She had to give Jake his due, he knew all the right moves. The only trouble was she wasn't interested. 'How did you get my telephone number? No—don't tell me,' she sighed. 'Melanie.'

'Right,' he chuckled.

'Was there anything else?' she asked distantly, just longing to go back to sleep. Melanie's dinner party hadn't just interrupted one day's work, usually she would have been thinking of getting up by this time, and would have been typing before ten o'clock. She always typed her own work, she found it easier that way. Besides, she doubted anyone else would be able to read her almost microscopic writing.

'Plenty,' Jake drawled, not at all put off by her cold manner. 'But I think it's a little early in the day for an obscene telephone call.'

A reluctant smile curved her lips. 'Don't you have to get to work?' She refused to show him how much he was disturbing her. His voice was so clear, so close, that it almost sounded as if he were in the room with her— in the bed!

'Thanks for reminding me,' he said ruefully. 'I'd like to tell you to stay just where you are until tonight, but I don't think you would agree.'

'You're right—I wouldn't.'

'Shame. Okay, Juliet, eight-thirty, right?'

'Jake!' she tried to catch him before he rang off.

'Yes?' he answered instantly. 'You aren't going to let me down, are you? I had to cancel an important engagement tonight so I could see you instead.'

'With Patricia Hall?' she queried sarcastically, feeling more awake by the second, remembering now that he was supposed to have a girl-friend.

'Melanie is a busy little bee, isn't she?' he taunted. 'I take it she was the one who supplied that bit of information.'

'You take it right. And if Patricia Hall thinks she has a claim on you I'd rather not get involved.'

'Pat doesn't have a claim on me, no woman does. We see each other when we're both free, which hasn't been very often lately. My engagement was with one of the guests scheduled to be on my show. I usually like to have at least one meeting with them before we record the show.'

'And who was it this time?' Her interest quickened in spite of herself, for she found her fellow writers a fascinating subject.

'Gregory James,' Jake laughed. 'He doesn't bear grudges.'

'I hope you're right,' she said dryly. 'Although it could be quite fun to see him take a swing at you in front of the camera.'

'That isn't nice, Juliet,' he chided teasingly.

'No,' she agreed, laughing.

'I'll see you later—when you can expect suitable retribution.'

Juliet lay back on the bed once he had rung off, wide awake now, her mind racing. Gregory James might not bear grudges, but she did, and in front of thousands of the public would be a perfect time to let Jake know who

she really was. The idea mushroomed and grew, until
she was sure it could work. It would take a little planning, good timing, and most of all, sheer nerve, but it
would be worth it just to see the embarrassed surprise
on Jake's face.

How to arrange it, that was the thing. She couldn't
approach Jake herself, that would give the whole game
away, so that left Michael. She wasn't sure he would
play along with something like this. It would be a
deliberate move on his part to make a fool of Jake, and
Michael was a businessman before he was her friend.
Not that she could blame him for that, she was far from
being the only author on his books, and Jake Matthews
had been known to ruin a book's sales with a few cutting
words, something no sensible publisher would want at
any cost.

Maybe Melanie could be persuaded to help; Michael
rarely denied his wife anything. But first of all she would
have to persuade Melanie!

'No,' her friend instantly refused once the idea was
outlined to her.

Somehow she had known her friend was going to say
that, had known the expensive lunch she had treated
her to would be a waste of her time and money. And
she had to admit that in the clear light of day, the fog of
sleep completely cleared from her brain, that it was a
childish idea. It could also have been harmful to her
career.

'I had a feeling you would say that,' she grimaced.
'Let's just forget the idea.'

'Michael would never stand for it,' Melanie nodded.
'Not with someone like Jake Matthews. Has he called
you yet? I gave him your number this morning.'

'I know. And the reason my number isn't in the book
is because I only want the people I personally give it to
to be able to use it.'

'Oh,' Melanie looked abashed. But not for long! 'But

you didn't mind my giving it to Jake, surely?'

'I minded,' Juliet said dryly. 'Especially when he called me in the middle of the night.'

'Don't exaggerate,' her friend smiled. 'He spoke to me at seven-thirty, so it must have been later than that.'

'Ten to eight is the middle of the night to me,' Juliet groaned. 'I don't think I've recovered from the shock yet. I usually manage to crawl out of bed just after nine, ready to start work at ten.'

'Lazy!' Melanie smiled. 'I always get up and eat breakfast with Michael at seven-thirty before he has to leave for work.'

'God!' she grimaced. 'And then what do you do for the rest of the day?'

Her friend shrugged, playing with the spoon in her coffee cup, their meal over. 'I keep busy,' she evaded.

'But how?'

'I shop, see friends, organise the staff. I keep busy,' she defended. 'We can't all be career-women. I happen to like making a home for Michael.'

'I didn't mean to sound critical.' Juliet touched Melanie's hand for forgiveness. 'We just seem to have come a long way from the time you were going to be the best singer in the world and I was going to be the personal assistant and mistress of a millionaire.'

Melanie giggled. 'You always did have a warped idea of love and marriage.'

Warped? Was it really? She had never thought so. She had a brain, she wanted to use it, and if that meant she could never have the ideal marriage Melanie seemed to have then that was the way it was going to be. Shopping, seeing friends, and organising a household for her husband's pleasure and comfort was not something she could settle for in her life. Writing was a fundamental part of her life now, and she couldn't live without it.

But she knew Melanie was happy, knew that she and

Michael were planning to start a family, but it just
hadn't worked out yet. But when it did Melanie was
going to make a wonderful mother. She wasn't so sure
her own maternal instinct was as strong. There was
something missing from her feminine make-up, the fundamental ingredient that made all her friends settle for
being a wife and mother while she still clung fiercely to
her independence, to her individuality. It seemed to her
that marriage was a series of compromises, that you
were never truly happy because you could never quite
have what you wanted, only what you and your partner
decided to have.

Most people would say her attitude was selfish, and
maybe it was, but at the moment she hadn't seen a way
of life that had more to offer.

'You'll forget this idea of going on Jake's show, won't
you?' Melanie frowned worriedly. 'I'm sure it could be
arranged but like I told you yesterday, underneath the
charm there beats a heart of pure steel. He would crucify
you, probably Michael too.'

'I'll forget it,' she agreed. 'But you'll admit it was a
good idea?' she said ruefully.

'Fantastic,' Melanie nodded. 'Although maybe you
won't think so after tonight, hmm?'

Juliet smiled. 'You're a romantic,' she scorned.

'So are you,' Melanie flushed. 'Underneath all that
hard-headed career-woman attitude.'

'And if it isn't just an attitude?'

'It is,' her friend said with certainty. 'I remember you
when you had dreams as silly as mine.'

'The only difference being you made yours come
true.'

'Yours still could——'

'No,' Juliet shook her head firmly. 'My dreams didn't
fit in with reality. Goodness,' she lightened her tone,
'we've become very serious all of a sudden! Do you
suppose we're getting old, we seem to have said a lot

of "I remembers" today?'

'Speak for yourself,' Melanie scorned. 'You're only as old as you feel, and I feel—oh, at least—twenty-four,' she grinned.

'Come on,' Juliet stood up, 'I'll drive you home.'

The idea of fooling Jake any more than she already had was mutually dropped. It had been a mad scheme that would probably have caused more trouble than it was worth. Besides, she had *Mason's Fortune* to think of. Maybe the critical Mr Matthews would like the sequel to *Mason's Heritage*. One could only hope.

The telephone was ringing when she let herself into her apartment and she hastily snatched up the receiver. 'Yes?' she said tersely, breathing heavily from her haste from the lift.

'I haven't interrupted your work, have I, dear?' her mother's voice came very clearly down the line.

Juliet had suspected that the caller was Jake Matthews, he was being very persistent, but she was relieved, if surprised, that it was her mother. 'I wasn't working, I've been out,' she explained, once again sitting down in the chair next to the telephone. If anything her mother chattered more than Melanie did!

'Anywhere nice?' her mother asked brightly.

'Just to lunch with Melanie. Is there anything wrong, Mother?' she asked sharply.

'Can't I just call my daughter to see how she is?' Her mother sounded indignant.

'It isn't something you usually do,' Juliet said dryly, easing her shoes off her feet, flexing the arches as she listened to her mother. Melanie had insisted on going round the shops for an hour before they had lunch, and her feet now ached.

'No, well, I—I wondered if I could stay with you overnight next Friday.'

'Next Friday?' she frowned. 'Why?'

'Really, Juliet, couldn't I just want to visit you?'

'No,' she said from experience.

'Honestly, Juliet——'

Her mother was as aware of the meaning of the word honesty as Michael was! 'What's happening next Friday?' she sighed, the prospect of her mother descending on her, even for a day, filling her with apprehension. She and her mother invariably clashed when they met, although they could be friends from a distance.

'Nothing is happening next Friday,' her mother answered impatiently. 'Have you forgotten, I'm going on holiday next Saturday?'

She was ashamed to say she had. Her mother was always flitting from one place to another, always in one country or another, financially secure and with a wanderlust that she settled every three or four months by visiting a country other than England.

'Where are you off to this time?' she asked resignedly.

'South Africa.'

'South Africa?' she repeated incredulously. 'Why South Africa?'

'I've heard it's very beautiful,' her mother defended.

'So have I. I just never imagined it would appeal to you.'

'Well, it does. And I'm taking your Aunt Josephine with me this time.'

Poor Aunt Josephine! Her mother's sister had lived with them when Juliet was a child, often taking care of her when her mother had gone off on her travels. It had surprised the whole family when Aunt Josephine had upped and moved to London fifteen years ago. Juliet's mother hadn't forgiven the other woman for years, although the two of them were now close again, and her mother often dragged the other woman off on her holidays with her. Juliet could only sympathise with her, although her good-natured Aunt Josephine didn't seem to mind.

'Why can't you stay with Aunt Josephine?' she queried suspiciously.

'If you don't want me to stay with you——'

'I didn't say that,' Juliet sighed. 'I just wondered what Aunt Josephine had done that you weren't going to stay with her.'

'She hasn't done anything,' her mother snapped impatiently, 'except get the decorators in. Honestly, Juliet, only your Aunt Josephine could decide to have her flat decorated the week before we go on holiday. The whole place will smell of paint,' she added disgustedly.

Her poor aunt would never hear the end of it! 'Friday night is fine by me. What time will you arrive?'

'Don't tie me down to times,' her mother said in a harassed voice. 'You know how I hate someone standing over me with a watch. Your father used to do it all the time.'

'Let's leave Daddy out of this, shall we?' Juliet said tightly.

'If you like,' her mother accepted lightly. 'Have either of your young men proposed to you yet?'

'No, and I don't want them to either.'

'There's no chance of your making me a grandmother, then?'

'I don't have to get married for that,' Juliet taunted.

'You'd certainly better! Juliet——'

'I'm only teasing you, Mother,' she said dryly.

'Well, don't tease about things like that. Your father would have been shocked to hear you talking like that.'

'Considering Daddy's been dead for seven years, and you've had two other husbands since then, I'm surprised you can still remember how my father would have reacted to anything!' Juliet drew in a controlling breath after her outburst. 'I'm sorry, Mother, that was uncalled for.' She bit her lip.

'Yes, it was,' her mother agreed with quiet dignity.

'I'm sorry,' she repeated abruptly.

'You've said that.'

'I—I'll see you next Friday, then?'

'Some time in the evening,' her mother confirmed distantly before ringing off.

Oh dear, she had done it again! She and her mother always argued, no matter how much she tried to hold back her resentment for her mother's other two marriages. Jim had been first, five years her mother's junior, and they had divorced after only two years of marriage. The break-up had come as no surprise to Juliet, the passes Jim made at her behind her mother's back showing her the marriage was not a success. Then had come Robert, eight years younger than her mother this time, although she had somehow managed to outlive him. Juliet lived in trepidation of being presented with a third stepfather, maybe even her contemporary in age this time!

The call from her mother had upset her, and now she somehow had to get into the mood for her evening out with Jake Matthews. Her work had gone to pot today, both her typing and her writing. She would have to make an early start tomorrow to make up for it, otherwise she would be getting behind her deadline, which wouldn't please Michael.

Dinner, Jake Matthews had said. But where? She had no idea how to dress for the evening, although like most sensible women she had the versatile 'little black dress' that was suitable for most occasions. She decided to play safe and wear that; its style was demure enough until you saw the low back, its length just below her knees.

She had a long soak in the bath first, enjoying a relaxing read. She loved to read, but her daily schedule was such that she rarely got to indulge in this pleasure. Today seemed to be an unexpected holiday for her, so she became involved in one of the paperbacks she had been promising herself she would read for ages.

She became so involved in the new Sidney Sheldon novel that she almost forgot to get ready for Jake Matthews' arrival at eight-thirty. She was reasonably pleased with her appearance, looking coolly attractive, her auburn hair newly washed and gleaming, her make-up light, her manner composed.

Jake arrived promptly at eight-thirty, his gaze appreciative as she opened the door to him. He was very dark and distinguished in a black evening suit and snowy white shirt, looking rakishly attractive.

'Come in,' she invited huskily.

'Thanks.' He closed the door behind him. 'I really didn't dream you, did I?' He shook his head almost dazedly.

'My mother would say no,' she told him lightly. 'She says I was a very difficult birth.' The steadiness of his direct gaze unnerved her. 'I—We both almost died.' Heavens, he had to stop looking at her like that! She could feel the hot colour flooding her cheeks.

'Thank God you didn't,' he groaned, pulling her effortlessly into his arms and gazing down at her for several timeless seconds. 'It's those eyes,' he spoke almost to himself. 'I've never seen eyes that colour before.'

Juliet licked her lips nervously, unable to break his gaze. 'I—My father had eyes the same colour.'

Jake shook his head. 'Not just that colour. Maybe a deep dark brown, but never the same colour. You're unique!'

'Of course I'm not,' she dismissed lightly, moving away from him. 'Shall we be on our way?' It was too confined here alone with him in her flat, too intimate, especially as he couldn't seem to stop looking at her.

'I've booked a table in a quiet little restaurant I know,' he held up her evening jacket for her. 'I thought we could talk.'

What about? As far as she knew they had nothing in

common except their love of books, and that was perhaps a subject they should stear clear of—she wouldn't
like them to get thrown out of this 'quiet little restaurant' for causing a scene. She couldn't agree with his
opinions, or the way he put those opinions across to the
public, and she wouldn't even pretend to do so.

But she needn't have worried, they seemed to talk
about every thing else but books, both of them staying
off the subject, whether consciously or unconsciously.

Jake was an entertaining companion, and had lots of
amusing stories that he related to her. Juliet couldn't
ever remember laughing so much in one evening, Ben
and Stephen never made her laugh like this.

But they didn't keep staring at her either, something
Jake did all the time. There were plenty of beautiful
women in the room, Jake's idea of a quiet little restaurant was vastly different from her own, but he seemed
not to notice any of them, keeping his attention
exclusively on her.

She began to relax as she drank the delicious wine he
had ordered with their meal, although he remained
unmoved by it, even the large brandy he had after their
meal not seeming to affect him. When she mentioned it
he gave a husky laugh.

'I have so many business lunches and dinners that
I'm afraid I'm not as susceptible to alcohol as I used to
be. Besides, I haven't really drunk as much as you think
I have, my wine glass was never empty when it was
refilled.'

No, it hadn't been, now she came to think about it.
Every time her own glass was refilled Jake's was only
topped up. 'You've made me drunk,' she accused indignantly.

'No, I haven't,' he smiled, his eyes deeply blue.
'Maybe a little happy, but not drunk. Melanie told me
you don't relax enough, so I——'

'Got me drunk,' she insisted.

'No,' Jake laughed. 'You're fine, really. And maybe you like me a little better now, hmm?'

'And maybe I don't,' she said crossly. 'You're going to look pretty stupid if I collapse halfway out of the restaurant.'

His eyes twinkled with humour. 'Do you think you might?'

'Well, I—I feel all right,' Juliet frowned. 'But you never can tell.'

'I can,' his mouth quirked. 'You'll make it outside.'

And she did, Jake's arm about her waist as he guided her. Surprisingly she didn't feel drunk, just happy as Jake had said she would. What a know-it-all he was!

'Do I get invited in for coffee tonight?' He turned in his seat after parking the car outside her apartment building.

She thought of her neat little flat, of the incriminating typewritten sheets she had locked away earlier this evening so that he shouldn't see them and realise she wrote for a living. No, she had left nothing lying about to point to her being Caroline Miles, although it was very late, too late really to ask him inside.

'You had coffee at the restaurant,' she pointed out.

'I happen to like coffee,' he mocked.

She wasn't sure inviting him in was a good idea, but it would look childish if she didn't. She was twenty-four years old, not sixteen, and should be perfectly capable of handling one amorous male. Lord, she was starting to sound like Sophie Mason now, the latest mistress of Mason House—and almost a century separated them!

'Make yourself comfortable,' she invited once they were inside her home. 'I'll just go and make the coffee.'

Jake eyed her mockingly. 'You didn't really think I came up here for coffee?'

Juliet put her jacket away in the hall closet. 'Whether you did or not, that's what you're getting.' She turned, only to find him suddenly dangerously close. 'Excuse me——' she made to walk past him, her eyes on a level with the cleft in his chin.

His arms came about her. 'Juliet . . .!'

She managed to extricate herself from his arms, moving a safe distance away—if there could be such a thing with this virilely attractive man! There was an aura about him, an air of sexual challenge, and it drew her like a magnet. But she had to be sensible. She already had two men in her life, a third would just be an unnecessary complication. Besides, Jake Matthews was the last man she wanted to become involved with.

'Coffee,' she insisted firmly.

He grimaced. 'Do I get to kiss you after that?'

'Perhaps.' She went through to the kitchen, conscious of him watching her. He was always watching her! 'Would you go and wait in the other room?' she requested irritably.

Jake leant back against one of the kitchen cabinets, his arms folded across his chest. 'I'm comfortable where I am.'

Juliet was far from being comfortable, her hands shaking slightly as she prepared the tray of coffee.

'Let me.' Jake picked up the tray once it was ready and carried it through to the lounge for her.

Just as she was about to sit down and pour the coffee the telephone rang. She frowned; who on earth could be calling this time of night?—it was after eleven. 'Help yourself,' she told Jake absently, picking up the telephone.

'If it's Melanie,' Jake drawled softly, 'tell her to call back in the morning when you might have more to tell her.'

Juliet turned her back on him, scowling heavily. She would have him out of her flat as soon as he had drunk his coffee! 'Yes?' she snapped into the receiver.

'Who's there with you, Juliet?' Ben asked tersely. 'Is it Stephen?'

'Ben!' Her face lit up with pleasure, not noticing the dark enquiring look Jake shot her way. 'When did you get back?'

'A few minutes ago. I told you I'd call you as soon as I got back to town. You didn't answer my question, is that Stephen there with you?'

'Er—no, it isn't Stephen. It's just a—a friend.' She studiously avoided looking at Jake. 'We were just having coffee.' She noticed Jake hadn't so much as touched the pot of coffee, his attention all on her.

'Another one,' Ben sighed. 'Stephen I can stand, but I don't like the idea of you going out with some other man.'

'Don't be silly,' she dismissed lightly. 'Did you have a good trip?'

'Not bad.' He seemed to relax. 'I'll tell you all about it when I see you. Are you free tomorrow?'

She glanced fleetingly at Jake, shivering at the intensity of his gaze, angry at the way he was blatantly listening to her end of the conversation, although he couldn't possibly have heard Ben's.

'Tomorrow sounds fine. Would you like me to cook you dinner?' He was bound to feel tired after his flight back from America, and he would feel even worse tomorrow once the jet-lag caught up with him. She doubted he would feel much like going out anywhere. Besides, she could do with a quiet evening at home herself.

'Lovely,' Ben accepted. 'About eight? I'll bring the wine.'

'I'll look forward to seeing you.' She rang off. 'That was Ben,' she told Jake needlessly.

'So I gathered,' he drawled, all humour gone now from his rugged features. 'Anyone I know?'

Juliet shrugged. 'His name is Ben Sheffield. He's——'

'Of Sheffield Engineering?' Jake asked tautly, sitting forward in his seat.

'Er—yes,' she nodded. 'Do you know him?' That was all she needed!

'Of him,' Jake corrected. 'He's the boy wonder in engineering, a self-made millionaire.'

At twenty-nine Ben ran and owned one of the more successful engineering firms, but he had done it the hard way, had worked his way up from nothing, making a success of a firm that had been falling into decline. And he still worked hard. He liked to play hard too, but Juliet resented Jake's derision on his behalf.

'He is very successful,' she agreed coolly. 'You didn't help yourself to coffee. Let me——'

'You were agreeing to see Sheffield tomorrow?' Jake interrupted abruptly.

'Yes.' She poured out the coffee anyway, drinking hers although Jake left his untouched.

'I had plans of my own for us tomorrow.'

'I'm sorry,' she looked at him steadily. 'You didn't say, and Ben——'

'Asked first,' he completed grimly, his eyes narrowed. 'How long have you known him?'

'About six months.'

'You didn't tell me you had a boy-friend,' he said tautly, his eyes glittering.

'Ben is male, and he's also a friend, so I suppose that makes him a boy-friend,' she answered coolly, the effects of the wine completely gone now. 'Although I doubt he would appreciate the description. And I didn't tell you because you didn't ask. The same way I didn't ask if you had a girl-friend.'

'But you know about Pat.'

'Only because Melanie told me. I certainly didn't ask her.'

'Because you weren't interested!'

'Not particularly,' she shrugged. 'You aren't drinking your coffee, Jake,' she added infuriatingly, putting down her own empty cup.

'I never wanted the damned coffee!' He stood up forcefully, pacing the room. 'Just why the hell did you go out with me?' He stood over her, his expression fierce.

She looked up at him with those calm sherry-coloured eyes he so admired. 'You asked me.'

'Hell!' He swore under his breath, pulling her roughly to her feet. 'If I don't soon kiss you . . .' he muttered with a groan, his head swooping and his lips claiming hers.

Once again she wasn't prepared for him to kiss her, and her mouth opened beneath the pressure of his as his arms about her waist arched her body up to meet his. His muscles were tense, his body like a hard wall, almost hurting her as he curved her against him. His mouth moved heatedly over hers, taking but giving pleasure in return, his hands moving restlessly across her back, his touch on her bare skin sending rivulets of pleasure down her spine. And still he kissed her, more deeply now, slowly tasting all the nectar she had to give.

Juliet clung to him weakly, feeling as if she had been taken over by a whirlwind, not even sure her feet were still on the ground, the world suddenly seeming at a crazy tilt.

Jake's lips moved to her throat with a satisfied sigh, probing the sensitive area just below her ear. 'I've wanted to do this ever since we parted last night,' he breathed raggedly. 'Do you have any idea how disturbing you are to a man's equilibrium?'

She was disturbing? Did he know how disturbing *he* was? Her heart was beating so loudly she could hear it, and Jake must know how rapidly it was beating too; his hand was lightly cupping her breast, gently massaging.

'I don't think I've heard anything that's been said to me today,' he continued ruefully, his forehead resting on hers. 'Did you know you had that effect on men?'

'No . . .'

'Well, you do. On me, anyway. Probably Ben too,' he added hardly.

'No,' she laughed lightly, dismissively. Her relationship with Ben was kept strictly to a light goodnight kiss, and that was the way they both liked it. Jake was right about Ben being a millionaire, he was, and he hated the female attention his sudden wealth had brought him. The two of them had met at one of Melanie's parties, naturally, and had decided to go out together for mutual protection. Unfortunately, Melanie had guessed the truth, and still continued to matchmake for Juliet, although Ben would have none of her schemes.

'Stephen, then,' Jake probed. 'Who is Stephen? Your brother?'

'He——' once again the telephone rang. 'I wonder who that can be?' she frowned.

Jake's arms dropped from about her, his sigh impatient. 'Probably Stephen,' he scowled.

She had a strange feeling he was right, and she picked up the receiver almost apprehensively.

'Was that Ben on the telephone just now?' Stephen asked without preliminary.

Oh dear, this was so embarrassing! 'Yes,' she replied huskily, not even daring to look at Jake.

'He's back, then,' Stephen said thoughtfully.

'Yes,' she confirmed.

'Great. I'll see if he wants a game of squash tomorrow,' he said cheerfully. 'No doubt he could use some exercise after all those business lunches.'

'No doubt,' she agreed, finally having glanced at Jake, to see his face like thunder. She doubted he had ever had this much competition before all in the same evening! And she wasn't sure it showed her in a good light. She knew that Ben and Stephen were both just friends, but Jake obviously wasn't drawing that conclusion.

'I suppose you'll be seeing him tomorrow,' Stephen sighed.

'Yes.'

'Damn! I wanted you to come to an important business meeting with me. You know what a diversion you are.'

'Yes,' she agreed dryly. Stephen was a business friend of Ben's, and the two of them had met through Ben. Stephen's intentions were just as casual as Ben's, and he was also just a friend as far as she was concerned. She had no doubt that either or both of them would deepen the relationship if she were willing but she had shown them from the first that she wasn't interested.

'Are you free on Saturday instead?' Stephen asked hopefully. 'I've been calling you all evening in the hope that I could get my invitation in before Ben. He came back early.'

'Yes,' she said huskily, seeing Jake was getting angrier and angrier by the minute.

'Hey, you sound a bit odd,' Stephen finally realised. 'And you've been out all evening,' he added thoughtfully. 'Have I interrupted something?'

Had he? Yes, perhaps. But she was glad he had. She had forgotten for a moment who Jake was, and it had been a lapse she could have paid dearly for.

She looked up at him with hard eyes, this time seeing none of the rugged attractiveness, the entertaining companion of the evening, seeing only the critic, the man who ripped a person's dreams apart with a few cruel words.

'No, you haven't interrupted anything,' she told Stephen steadily. 'And Saturday sounds fine. Will you be able to change your plans to then? They sound very—interesting.' She made her voice sound deliberately provocative, instantly seeing Jake's mouth set in a thin angry line, his eyes contemptuous.

'I'll have a damn good try,' Stephen said enthusiastically. 'I'll call you some time tomorrow and let you know what the arrangements are.'

'Fine.' Once again she rang off, aware that Jake must be getting the worst possible impression of her. Let him!

'Stephen?' he said grimly.

'Yes,' she shrugged.

'My God,' he sighed, 'you didn't tell me I had to get into a line-up for you!'

His tone was so insulting that it couldn't be mistaken for anything else, and Juliet's eyes sparkled with her own anger. 'You didn't ask,' she snapped.

'Are there any more I should know about, or is there just Ben and Stephen?' His mouth twisted contemptuously.

'Talk about double standards!' she scorned. 'I suppose it would be all right for you to be seeing two other women?'

'I didn't say that——'

'You didn't need to,' she cut in angrily. 'I've had one date with you, Mr Matthews, as far as I'm concerned one too many, and that certainly doesn't give you any right to judge me.'

His eyes glittered like chips of blue glass. 'And just now?'

'Just now?' she scorned. 'You rate no better and a damn sight lower as a lover than a lot of men I know.'

'Why, you little——!' He drew in a steadying breath. 'I'd better leave,' he said grimly.

'Yes, you had,' she agreed tightly.

He turned on his heel and slammed out of the apartment, leaving a white-faced Juliet staring after him.

It wasn't the things he had said that had upset her, or his obvious contempt for what he believed to be her promiscuous behaviour. No, it was the knowledge that she knew she had lied when she said he rated no better and a damn sight lower as a lover than other men she had known. She had never taken a lover, but she knew that tonight she had been dangerously close to it—and with Jake Matthews!

· CHAPTER THREE

IT was a relief to get down to some work the next day. At least while she was working she couldn't think of Jake. Not that she wanted to think about him, but she had never had any man treat her with such contempt before, and it had hurt.

She was aware that the telephone calls, first from Ben, and then from Stephen, had looked very incriminating, but Jake hadn't even given her a chance to explain herself.

This morning she determinedly put Jake Matthews from her mind, and thought only of Sophie Mason and the way she coped with her suddenly impotent husband from a riding accident after the birth of their two children, the way he often became violent, insanely jealous of any man who looked at her.

She felt sorry for Sophie Mason, caught in the restrictions of the Victorian era, society at its strictest, when the idea of separation or divorce was looked on most unfavourably. The fact that Sophie Mason had brought the fortune to the Mason family that the book's title referred to was immaterial. When she married Gerald Mason all her wealth, her very person, became her husband's property.

Juliet couldn't have stood such restrictions herself, and some of her own rebellion came out in Sophie's personality. Sophie was also one of the few Victorian women who had enjoyed a good sexual relationship with her own husband, something that only added to Gerald's jealousy when that side of their marriage broke down.

Mason's Fortune, like *Mason's Heritage*, had some

sexual scenes, something that had prompted Jake Matthews' scathing comment about Caroline Miles 'reliving the memories of her lost youth'. She wasn't reliving anything; those passages came purely from imagination, were completely fictional. But Michael had informed her that books without some sexual accounts, tastefully written of course, just didn't sell nowadays. It seemed the whole world had gone sex crazy!

Juliet had agreed to include these scenes, although she kept them to a minimum, and she didn't particularly enjoy writing them. But *Mason's Heritage* had sold, and she knew Jake Matthews' mention of 'memories of lost youth' hadn't hurt those sales.

Now she seemed to have backed Sophie into a corner, had to decide whether or not she should take a lover or remain faithful to her impotently violent husband. Juliet believed in fidelity herself, and it went against the grain to allow Sophie to take a lover. And yet Sophie was still a young and beautiful woman, barely thirty, and couldn't be expected to forgo the pleasures of her body for a man it was no longer possible to love, whose violence was becoming unbearable.

When the doorbell rang and interrupted her quandary she didn't know whether to groan her impatience for the work lost, or to sigh her relief. The latter, she finally decided. She could face the problem of Sophie tomorrow.

When she opened the door to Melanie she was no longer sure of that relief. Melanie was sure to ask personal questions—and she wouldn't leave until she had answers.

But for once Melanie had other things on her mind, a warm glow about her that was soon explained. 'I'm nine weeks pregnant!' she announced excitedly.

'That's wonderful!' Juliet hugged her friend, genuinely pleased for her. 'Does Michael know?'

Melanie nodded, seeming unable to stop smiling. 'I

called him at the office. He wanted to come straight home,' she giggled. 'I told him I have another seven months to go yet, he can start worrying then. He'll probably be bored with the whole thing by then. And so will I,' she grimaced.

'You'll love it all,' Juliet laughed.

Melanie pulled a face, as she sat down. 'I feel sort of strange,' she admitted ruefully. 'A bit as if I no longer belong to myself.'

'I suppose it's only natural,' Juliet soothed, having no idea how pregnant women felt.

'You think so?' Melanie said hopefully. 'I feel excited, and yet I feel scared too. Do you think he'll like me?'

'Who?' Juliet frowned her puzzlement. She had never seen Melanie like this before, uncertain and frightened. Did motherhood do that to you?

'The baby. Do you think——'

'Melanie!' she chided laughingly. 'It may not be a boy.'

'It will be,' Melanie said with certainty. 'After all this time of waiting it has to be.'

'If you say so. Would you like some tea?' Her offer accepted, Juliet went into the kitchen to make it. Melanie's pregnancy was wonderful news, and her friend was obviously pleased about it, although it had unnerved her too.

'So what about you?' Melanie asked as they drank their tea.

She had known it had to come, although she had hoped Melanie's condition would keep her mind off Jake Matthews. She should have known better.

'Well, I'm not pregnant, if that's what you mean,' she teased.

'Juliet!'

'I'm working hard.'

Her friend sighed impatiently. 'I want to know if you had a good time last night.'

'Very nice,' she replied primly.

'Are you seeing Jake again?'

'No,' she could reply with certainty.

'Oh.' Melanie looked disappointed. 'I felt sure the two of you would like each other.'

'Well, we don't.'

'But you went out with him!'

Yes, and she was still trying to work out why she had done it. At the time perhaps she had had visions of shouting 'Surprise! You just kissed Caroline Miles'. But what would be the point of that? Jake had the power to ruin her career, and it would be better in future if she stayed away from him. Her impetuousness would get her in serious trouble one of these days. If it hadn't already! But there was no reason why she and Jake should ever meet professionally; she wasn't one of those authors who sought out publicity, in fact the opposite.

It seemed to her there had never been a time when she hadn't written, stories for other children when she was younger, and attempts at thrillers when she was older. She had even sent several of her earlier attempts to publishers—not Michael, because she hadn't known him then—and had them rejected. It hadn't been until she sat down with Michael one evening and he had discussed the possibility of her writing a book of a Yorkshire family from the early 1800s. *Poldark* had just been shown on television, and Michael's company wanted to publish a book along similar lines in a different setting and with more concentration on the different generations. It had seemed a big undertaking at the time, especially for a newcomer, but Michael's confidence in her as a writer had been unshakeable. It had taken her eighteen months to write *Mason's Heritage*, and quite a bit of rewriting later, much to her surprise, it had been accepted for publishing.

But she still shied away from any form of publicity, preferring to keep her anonymity. She could imagine

nothing worse than going down to the local supermarket
and being recognised. Or perhaps she could. Going into
Marks & Spencers to buy her underwear and the girl on
the till knowing she was Caroline Miles!

'It was a mistake, Melanie,' she answered her friend.
'And one we both realised.'

'Yes, but—You didn't tell him about Ben and
Stephen?' Melanie exclaimed in dismay.

She pulled a face. 'Let's just say he knows about
them.'

'And he didn't like it,' Melanie said with certainty.

Juliet bristled angrily. 'He has no right to either like
or dislike it.'

'Of course he does——'

'We've had one date, Melanie. And I certainly didn't
object to this Patricia Hall you told me about.' She
remembered Jake's anger because she *hadn't*.

'That's because there's nothing to object to,' her
friend said awkwardly. 'I—I was a little out of date on
that. They haven't been out together for months.'

So Jake had been telling the truth about that. But
that still didn't mean she was his exclusive property.
Then why did she suddenly feel guilty about agreeing to
see Ben and Stephen in front of him? She didn't, of
course she didn't!

'That doesn't change anything,' she told Melanie
firmly.

'If only you wouldn't insist on going out with Ben
and Stephen. It's a complete waste of time.'

Her mouth twisted mockingly. 'Anything that doesn't
lead to marriage is a waste of time in your eyes. I happen
to enjoy the time I spend with them. And I don't intend
getting married,' she added vehemently. 'Not for love,
anyway.'

'That's silly——'

'That's fact, Melanie,' Juliet insisted abruptly. 'Loving
someone means you're completely at their mercy, and I

don't intend letting any man have that much power in my life. If Ben or Stephen ever asked me to marry them I might even consider saying yes, because I know I have their respect.'

'Respect doesn't give you happiness.'

'And neither does love!' she said fiercely, her sherry-coloured eyes glittering. 'Love is a weakening emotion, and I don't ever intend to let it weaken me.'

Melanie shook her head. 'You have it all wrong, Juliet. Love isn't like that. I know you were hurt in the past——'

'I wasn't hurt,' she stood up forcefully, to clear away their tea things, 'I just grew up in a hurry. Now can we please drop the subject? Jake Matthews really isn't worth it.'

Her friend frowned at her. 'You don't think so?'

'No, I don't,' she replied firmly.

Melanie shrugged. 'I think you're making a mistake, but——'

'Enough,' Juliet cut her friend off laughingly. They had become altogether too serious in the last few minutes, and about Jake Matthews of all people, a man who wasn't particularly important to either of them. 'Let's talk about something else, like the baby. Have you thought of any names yet?'

'It's a bit soon, I haven't even discussed it with Mich—Well, yes,' Melanie admitted at Juliet's knowing look, 'I have thought of a few, but——'

'I thought you might have done,' Juliet chuckled. 'Well, don't keep me in suspense!'

Melanie looked sheepish. 'You aren't really interested in babies.'

She hadn't been, she had to admit it. But somehow knowing her best friend was pregnant made the whole subject more interesting. Besides, it rankled slightly that Melanie should so dismiss her interest, it was almost like dismissing her femininity. And she was feminine—wasn't she?

'Tell me,' she encouraged stiltedly.

'Well ... I thought maybe Martha for a girl, and Josiah for a boy.' Melanie looked almost pleadingly at Juliet.

Juliet had trouble holding back her grimace. She hated the fashion of the moment of using old-fashioned names, pitying the children who would have to grow up with them. And how could you possibly call a little baby Martha or Josiah!

'Martha is pretty,' she compromised, not wanting to hurt Melanie's feelings.

'Mm, I'm not sure,' her friend said thoughtfully. 'Still, we have plenty of time to sort that out. I'd better get home now. I have to lie down for an hour, the doctor wants me to take things easy for the next few weeks— high blood-pressure or something like that.' She stood up. 'You know how I hate forced inactivity,' she grimaced. 'Still, if it's for the good of the baby. The baby has to come first. I suppose it's always like that when you have children.'

A thought suddenly occurred to Juliet, a way of solving the problem of Sophie without involving a third person. Children did have a way of coming first, especially in Sophie's time, so it would be only natural for a woman to expend all her time and emotion on her children. Sophie had one son, sent to boarding school, of course, like his father before him, but her daughter Emily was kept at home, like most girls her education not being felt to be important. Sophie could change all that. Emily could even become a Suffragette later on. And if this idea failed Sophie could always take a lover later in the book.

'Melanie, I think I love you,' she hugged her surprised friend. 'You've just helped me out of a tricky problem,' she explained the situation of Sophie to Melanie.

'It would have been more interesting if she'd taken a

lover,' Melanie scorned.

'I'll keep that as a standby.' She quirked a mocking eyebrow. 'And should you be talking that way in front of the baby?'

'What ba—Don't be silly,' Melanie scolded. 'He probably doesn't even have ears yet.'

'Don't you know?' Juliet teased. What she knew about babies, about children in general, could have been written on a picture postcard, since she was an only child herself, with no inclination to have any of her own. Which meant she would have to do even more research, since she intended to cover Emily's childhood quite extensively. It was mainly the research problem that made the *Mason* books so long and drawn out to write. One thing wrong, one mistake made by her that missed her editor's attention too, and the whole book could become a farce.

'I don't know yet,' her friend defended, 'but I will. I went out and bought half a dozen books on the development of babies, and bringing up a child.'

Juliet grinned. 'And they'll all tell you something totally different.'

'No doubt,' Melanie grimaced. 'But I'd better read them now, while it's all so new and interesting. By the time I'm seven or eight months pregnant I'll probably just be wishing it was all over.'

'Pessimist!' Juliet laughed.

'Realist,' Melanie corrected. 'Okay, okay, I can see you're pushing me out of the door. Do I get commission for all this help I'm giving you?'

'Ask Michael,' Juliet grinned. 'But I think the answer might be no. And I'm not pushing you out of the door, I just——'

'Want to get back to work,' her friend finished dryly. 'I'm glad I could be of help. And if Jake should call— —'

Juliet's humour faded at the mention of Jake, her

expression shuttered. 'He won't,' she said with certainty.

'But if he should——'

'He won't.' Just at that moment the telephone rang. 'That isn't him,' she sighed at Melanie's knowing look.

'I bet it is.'

'No,' she shook her head. 'Wait and see if you like.' She moved to pick up the receiver, recognising the voice on the line instantly. 'Hello, Stephen,' she greeted warmly, acknowledging Melanie's sticking-out tongue with a similar gesture of her own, and waving briefly as her friend quietly left.

'Is tomorrow still on?' Stephen wanted to know.

'If you managed to arrange it, yes.'

'Oh, great!' he enthused. 'My place, seven-thirty. Shall I call for you?'

'I don't think that will be necessary, I know the way,' Juliet smiled. 'Did you manage to contact Ben?'

'I'm just off to meet him now. How come I never get invited to dinner?' he added in a mock hurt.

Juliet laughed; this teasing was just what she needed as a balm to her dented ego. After the way Jake Matthews had stormed out of here last night she needed a little boost!

Ben was his usual lighthearted self when he arrived later that evening, dressed as casually as she was, in denims and shirt, handing her the wine as he made himself comfortable in one of the armchairs.

She wasn't a fantastic cook, but then she wasn't a bad one either! The chicken in wine sauce was nicely cooked, accompanied by baby new potatoes and fresh mixed vegetables, and there was a Black Forest gâteau for dessert, Ben's favourite, followed by cheese.

'So—who was he?' he asked as they relaxed in the lounge, the debris from the meal cleared away, Ben enjoying a brandy while Juliet sipped her coffee.

His question came as a surprise. Seconds earlier they

had been discussing the success of Ben's business trip, and now his sharp mind had gone off on a different tangent.

'Who was who?' She was genuinely puzzled.

'The man you had here last night.' He watched her steadily, a tall, dark-haired man, with the body of an athlete and the rugged good looks of a film star. It was his good looks as much as anything that attracted women to him wherever he went, but the suddenness of his wealth had taken away his ability to judge whether a woman genuinely wanted him or his money. One day, Juliet was sure, he would find the women he knew genuinely loved him, but in the meantime she was glad to be counted as one of his friends.

Colour flooded her cheeks, and she knew that colour would clash with her auburn tresses. 'Just a friend,' she dismissed, as she had last night when he asked.

Ben frowned. 'Stephen said he was still here when he telephoned you.'

She gave a light laugh. 'Considering he only called five minutes after you that isn't surprising.'

'So, who was he?'

'No one you know.' She was curiously reluctant to talk about Jake Matthews. It had been a mistake to go out with him in the first place, the less she said about it the better.

Ben shrugged. 'Then it won't hurt if you tell me.'

'Ben, really——'

'Oh, come on, Juliet. It isn't going to hurt you to tell me the man's name.'

She gave an impatient sigh. But like Ben said, it couldn't hurt just to tell him the name. 'It was Jake Matthews,' she revealed reluctantly.

His brown eyes narrowed thoughtfully, the cleft in his chin more pronounced. He really was incredibly handsome, Juliet thought smilingly, much too good-looking

to be wasting his time on a mere friendship with a
woman.

'The critic?' he said slowly.

'That's right,' she nodded.

'Oh well, if it was business . . .'

'It wasn't,' she instantly denied. 'Really, Ben, I don't
see what difference it makes whether or not it was a
business dinner.'

'It matters to me,' he said indignantly.

'Why?'

'Why? Because—Well——'

Juliet sighed. 'You're the last person I expected to
play the part of outraged lover,' she mocked.

'I'm not outraged——'

'You aren't a lover either,' she teased.

He gave a rueful smile. 'I thought Stephen and I were
the only men you went out with.'

'Well, you thought wrong.'

'Stephen doesn't like the idea either, you know.'

'Tough!'

Ben frowned his consternation. 'Why won't you ever
take us seriously? Goodness knows we've been seeing you
long enough.'

Her eyes widened mockingly. 'You want me to get
serious about *both* of you?'

He stood up, his hands thrust in his denims' pockets
as he paced the room, the overhead light making the
gold of the medallion he wore glisten brightly. 'You
know I didn't mean it that way,' he sighed impatiently.
'But we thought you would have shown a preference for
one of us by now.'

Juliet looked at him searchingly. He was really serious
about this. 'You're being ridiculous,' she said irritably.
'You know we've only ever been friends——'

'Because that's what you wanted,' he cut in. 'But I've
missed you while I've been away this time. I don't want
to be just a friend any more.'

'But I can't give you any more than that,' she told him impatiently.

'Jake Matthews——'

'Him either!' her eyes flashed. 'If my going out with him for one evening has prompted this show of possessiveness, let me put your mind at rest. I won't be seeing him again.'

Relief flickered in his eyes. 'You won't?'

'No.'

'Oh.'

'No more half-declarations of love, or claims of missing me?' she asked tongue-in-cheek.

'Juliet——'

'I'm only teasing you, Ben,' she laughed. 'Is Stephen going to act the same way tomorrow?' she groaned.

'Well . . .'

'Is he?' she grimaced.

'He could be,' Ben revealed reluctantly.

'Oh God!' she raised her eyes heavenwards. 'You two are acting like a couple of children. I only spent one evening with the man!'

Ben frowned down at her. 'But you've never done it before.'

'I don't usually have the time,' she taunted his and Stephen's monopoly of her time.

'How did you meet him?'

'Guess!'

'Not Melanie,' he groaned. 'Lord, how she loves to interfere in your life!'

'She won't have so much time for it in future.' She told him about the coming baby. 'I think that should keep her busy for a while.'

'I hope so. And you're sure there's no chance of your loving either Stephen or myself?'

'Very sure,' she smiled.

'Maybe if I kissed you . . .'

'You could try,' she said dryly. 'But I don't think it would do any good.'

Ben pulled her effortlessly to her feet, his hands linked loosely at the base of her spine as he held her to him. 'You really would make me a good wife, Juliet,' he told her huskily. 'Beautiful, bright, sexy——'

'And best of all, rich in my own right and so not after your money,' she taunted.

He smiled. 'There is that.'

'I'm sure.' Her arms were up about his neck. 'How about that kiss?' she invited.

His eyes widened. 'You really want me to?'

'Why not?' she shrugged.

Ben looked as if he could hardly believe his luck, and his head lowered and his mouth claimed hers.

All the time he was kissing her, bringing his undoubted experience to bear, she was aware of comparing him to Jake Matthews. And there was *no* comparison. Much as she hated to admit it, Ben's kiss was no more than pleasant, and for all that she liked him his mouth on hers evoked none of the consuming fire that a cynically mocking mouth on hers had.

'Relax,' Ben urged against her throat. 'Let your feelings flow.'

Her feelings were 'flowing', and Ben's kiss had done nothing for her. 'Kiss me again,' she urged, desperate to erase compelling lips on hers, long sensitive hands roaming caressingly over her body.

Ben's mouth once again claimed hers, and she could tell he was putting everything he had into the kiss, his mouth moving erotically against hers, tasting, devouring—and none of it meant a thing to her. It was as if she were clinically dissecting every moment, her thoughts completely removed from her body.

He moved back with a sigh. 'I'm not even touching you, am I?' he shook his head.

'I'm sorry, Ben,' she gently touched his rigid jaw. 'I'm sure hundreds of women would just love you to kiss them . . .'

'But not you.' He let her go completely, moving back to sit in the armchair. 'I wonder if Stephen will have any better luck tomorrow.'

She grimaced. 'You think he'll try?'

He grinned. 'I'm sure of it. We have a bet on which one of us can actually get you to respond.'

Juliet knew she should be angry, and yet somehow she wasn't. Ben and Stephen were like brothers to her, and she just couldn't be angry with them. 'You two are incorrigible!' She tried to sound stern, and knew she had failed, bursting out laughing. 'What would you have done if I'd taken you seriously just now?' she sobered. 'And I could have done—you wouldn't make a bad husband either.'

'Thanks! And if you had taken me seriously I would have been proud to have you as my wife. You're everything I would ever want.'

'But do you love me?'

'Love?' he grimaced. 'I'm beginning to wonder if it exists.'

Juliet shook her head, her sherry-coloured eyes dark. 'I don't think we would have had a very successful marriage—two cynics in one family wouldn't be a very good idea.'

'Probably not,' he agreed cheerfully. 'Your boy-friend's on the box now, by the way.'

'Boy-friend . . .?' she frowned. 'Oh, you mean Jake Matthews.' She glanced at her wrist-watch. 'So he is. Would you mind if I switched it on? Purely out of professional interest, of course,' she added at his sharp look.

'Go ahead,' he invited. 'I should be going now, anyway. It's been a long week, I could do with some sleep.'

Juliet didn't object, she would rather sit and watch the programme on her own anyway. 'And tell Stephen not to continue with the bet,' she warned as she saw him to the door. 'Or I might just accept him,' she teased.

Ben kissed her lightly on the lips. 'Marriage was my idea,' he admitted huskily. 'I really would have liked it.'

'Thank you.' She reached up and kissed him on the cheek. 'I'm very flattered.'

'But unmoved by my plea,' he said dryly.

She laughed lightly. 'Don't worry, I'll dance at your wedding—to someone else.'

Jake Matthews' programme was half over by the time she returned to the lounge and switched on the television. The programme was always shown live, and with Jake in charge the likelihood of anything going wrong was highly remote. Occasionally Juliet had seen the guest author become a little agitated by Jake's criticism, but it had never actually come to blows—although tonight could be another matter.

Gregory James was obviously annoyed about Jake's derogatory comments about *Devil's Dare*, and his attitude was aggressive. Juliet could only marvel at the way Jake handled him, almost having the renowned author agreeing with his criticism by the end of the programme.

But she shouldn't really have been surprised; hadn't Jake handled her in much the same way, evoked a physical response from her even though she had felt sure she would remain immune to him.

She knew that he had, knew that he was an expert when it came to controlling people and their emotions. Thank goodness, she would never have to see him again!

When the doorbell rang just after twelve o'clock she didn't know whether to be angry or alarmed, getting out of bed to pull on her robe, her hair in disorder about her make-upless face. *No one* visited this time of night.

Jake Matthews did! Still wearing the navy blue three-piece suit he had worn for his television programme, he looked dark and attractive, his eyes narrowing as he looked at her state of undress.

'Am I interrupting anything?' he drawled.

'Inter——? Certainly not!' Oh dear, she sounded prudish! It was perfectly natural for a woman of her age to go to bed with a man if she wanted to, most of her single friends did it all the time. 'Did you want something?' she asked stiltedly.

His eyes openly mocked her, his mouth quirked into a smile. 'What a question to ask me when you're dressed like that!'

'I suppose it was rather stupid,' she sighed. 'Did you want to come in?' Her tone was uninviting.

'So I'm not interrupting anything?'

'Only my sleep,' she snapped, turning back into the lounge, leaving it up to him to follow her.

Which he did, chuckling as he closed the door, his long legs soon bringing him through to the lounge. 'Sheffield must have left early.' He looked pointedly around the empty room.

Juliet's mouth thinned at his taunting tone, tucking the robe about her bare legs as she sat down. 'It is after twelve,' she told him stiffly, wondering what on earth he was doing here, any time of day or night. She could have sworn she wouldn't be seeing him again. Obviously she had misjudged his determination.

'So it is.' He gave a cursory glance at the plain gold watch on his wrist, the metal appearing brighter against the darkness of his skin, a fine sheen of dark hair against his firm skin. 'Mind if I sit down?'

'Feel free,' she invited waspishly, sighing her impatience as he stretched his long length out in one of the armchairs.

He studied her for several embarrassing minutes. 'I somehow thought you would look different from what you do when you go to bed.'

The fact that he had thought about it at all caused an angry sparkle to her sherry-coloured eyes. 'No one looks that glamorous when they go to bed!'

'I've seen a few . . .' His mouth quirked. 'But we won't go into that. And I'll admit that it was the *way* you look when you go to bed that surprised me, but my comment wasn't meant critically.' He was totally relaxed, not looking at all like a man who had spent a busy day and night at a television studio. 'I had somehow pictured you in a serviceable cotton nightdress. Instead of which, unless my eyes deceive me, you're wearing a sheer lace nightgown.'

She flushed her resentment of his scrutiny. 'I'm sure you didn't come here to discuss my night attire.' She resisted the impulse to pull her robe over the visible swell of her firm breasts, looking at him unflinchingly.

'Maybe not,' his eyes teased. 'But you have to admit it's an interesting subject.'

'Not to me,' she said tightly.

'Probably not,' he smiled. 'But I find it very— interesting.'

'Mr Matthews——'

He sobered. 'I'm sure we progressed to Jake last night.'

'Possibly. But——'

'Definitely,' he corrected. 'Juliet, I came to apologise.'

She blinked at him dazedly. 'Apologise?'

Her surprise seemed to amuse him. 'I can tell you didn't expect that,' he laughed. 'But my behaviour last night was ridiculous, to say the least.'

'I couldn't agree more!'

'I had a feeling you would say that.'

'I'm glad I'm so predictable,' she snapped.

'You aren't predictable at all, that's the trouble.' His mouth twisted ruefully. 'Finding out about Ben and Stephen threw me for a while. I don't know why it should have done, you're too beautiful to be on your own.'

'Thank you!' Her tone bordered on sarcasm.

'I know you're angry at me——'

'I'm tired.' She stood up abruptly. 'I'd like to get back to bed. You've made your apology, now I think I would like you to go.'

He didn't move so much as a muscle. 'How was your evening with Sheffield?' he asked casually.

She looked down at him frustratedly. 'It was very nice, thank you.'

'But he doesn't sleep here.'

She drew in an angry breath. 'Obviously not.'

'How about Stephen?'

'Not him either. Now would you mind going?' She moved to the door.

Jake moved too, coming up behind her, his hands on her arms pulling her back against him. 'How about me?' he said huskily.

Juliet spun round, at once wishing she hadn't as she was moulded against him. She quickly averted her eyes. 'How about you what?' she asked tightly, aware of everything about this man, his tangy aftershave, the potency of his animal magnetism.

'Will I be allowed to sleep here?'

Her head went back. 'No, you won't——'

Coolly moist lips moved over hers, sensually so, making a mockery of Ben's kiss earlier. This man's kisses were everything she remembered, and more, and excitement unwillingly built up within her.

'You were saying?' he murmured against her throat, his lips probing every shadowed curve.

Juliet swallowed hard. 'I don't have men—staying here.' Was that squeaky sound really her voice?

'Never?' His mouth returned to the edge of hers, his tongue caressing along the edge of her lower lip.

'N-never,' she said shakily.

'Maybe I'll be able to change that,' he suggested throatily, his eyes a deep, exciting blue.

'No . . .' She shook her head, pushing at his chest.

'Yes, Juliet!' His arms tightened about her. 'What are you so afraid of that last night you had to resort to insulting me to get me to leave, and tonight you're fighting me to get the same result?'

'I'm not afraid of anything!' Her anger gave her the strength to wrench away from him. 'You just don't attract me,' she added scornfully, her body tensed for further physical contact from him. 'Now I've asked you to leave,' her eyes blazed in her fury. 'But if you won't leave of your own accord then I'll just have to call the police to make you leave.'

Jake shook his head, not at all perturbed by her threat. 'You really are a fiery woman,' he mocked. 'I never know what you're going to do or say next.'

She walked over and wrenched the door open. 'Would you just leave?'

'If you insist,' he nodded, but took his time about joining her at the door.

He stopped at her desk on the way past, picking up one of the typewritten sheets she had left there for correcting. Juliet gasped, closing the door before rushing over to snatch the sheet of paper out of his hand, opening a drawer and pushing all the typewritten sheets inside.

Jakes eyebrows rose. 'What was that?'

'It—I——'

'It looked like a manuscript,' he frowned.

'I—er—Yes, it was.' She gave a light laugh, leaning back against the desk so that the drawer couldn't be opened. 'I remembered you'd mentioned that perhaps you—that you might look at that old manuscript for me,' she hastily invented. 'So I—I looked it out.' She gave him a bright, meaningless smile.

He gave a throaty laugh, and took her in his arms

once more. 'So you intended seeing me again all the time,' he mocked gently.

'I——' She shrugged. 'I wasn't sure.' Conceited idiot!

'But you got the manuscript out anyway.' He kissed along the line of her jaw.

'Er—yes.' She should never have gone out with this man, never have got involved with him! Lying went against her nature, and she despised herself for doing it, but she had her career to think about.

'Can I take it with me now?'

'No! I mean,' she licked her lips nervously, 'I was just doing a few alterations to it.'

'I see,' he nodded. 'In that case perhaps I can take it with me on Sunday?'

'Sunday?' she gave him a startled look.

His expression darkened. 'You don't already have a date for Sunday, do you?'

'No. But——'

'Good. You have now.' He gave her a brief kiss before releasing her. 'We can discuss your dropping Ben and Stephen then.'

'Dropping them? But——'

'Go back to bed now, Juliet,' he gently touched her cheek. 'I'll see you on Sunday morning, nice and early.'

'Oh, but——'

' 'Night, darling.' The door closed softly behind him, and a few seconds later she heard the descent of the lift.

Now what had she done? Not only was she going to see him on Sunday, she was also supposed to give him a non-existent manuscript!

CHAPTER FOUR

'You aren't your usually sparkling self this evening,' Stephen complained in a whisper.

'Sorry!' she turned to snap at him. 'I didn't realise I was here to be a sideshow.'

He looked visibly taken aback by her attack, an uncomfortable flush colouring his cheeks. At twenty-seven Stephen Blake was being groomed to take over his father's engineering firm, Stephen Senior, making him work his way up from the bottom of the company, showing no favouritism because he was his son.

It had been their mutual interest in engineering that had first brought Ben and Stephen together, and the two of them were now firm friends. Stephen wasn't as good-looking as Ben, with his overlong blond hair and twinkling blue eyes, but he was fun to be with, and she usually enjoyed the time she spent with him.

Tonight was different. After her late night meeting with Jake Matthews she was feeling tired and irritable. Her work wasn't going well, nowhere near the schedule she had set for herself, and she wasn't in the mood to be charming and entertaining to Stephen's dinner guests; the other two men's admiration irritated her. When Stephen had said he wanted her here as a diversion she hadn't thought she would be the only woman present with three men!

'If you're annoyed about this stupid bet Ben and I had——'

'I'm not,' she interrupted, not having given it a second thought, dismissing it from her mind, as it deserved to be dismissed.

'We only did it for a joke.' He looked at her anxiously.

'I know that.' She squeezed his hand. 'Would you mind if I went home, Stephen? I have a headache,' she invented.

He groaned his dismay. 'What do I do with those two?' He looked over to where the two businessmen were in conversation.

'Take them to a strip show or something,' she snapped, slamming her glass down on the table, as the headache rapidly became a reality. 'Isn't that what jaded businessmen like to see when they come up to London?' she said coldly.

'Juliet——'

'I have to go, Stephen. Please make my excuses.' She turned on her heel and walked out to the door.

Stephen caught up with her just as she was leaving, an anxious frown on his youthful face. 'Juliet, what have I done?' he asked worriedly. 'If I've insulted you in some way . . .'

'You haven't,' she reassured him, touching his arm gently. 'I'm just uptight. The book isn't going as it should, and—well, I think I'm just a bit down.'

'I understand,' he patted her hand. 'I'll call you tomorrow.'

'No! I mean, I—er—I thought I might go out for the day.' The last thing she needed was either Ben or Stephen telephoning when Jake Matthews was there!

'Good idea,' he smiled. 'Just take things easy. You work too hard.'

She gave a tight smile. 'I'll call you in the week, okay?'

'Right,' he nodded, kissing her lightly on the cheek. 'Take care.'

She still couldn't relax when she got home. Just what was wrong with her? Since she had met Jake Matthews her behaviour had become very erratic, unrecognisably so. She couldn't ever remember letting anyone else

bother her as much as he did. He had upset the even
tenor of her life to such a degree that she was snapping
and snarling at everyone.

In the six months that she had known Ben and
Stephen her relationship with them both had continued
on an even keel, now in the space of two days she had
turned down a marriage proposal from Ben and had
argued with Stephen. She was suddenly dissatisfied with
her life, bored with the daily pattern she had made for
herself, and her writing was suffering because of it. She
had kept to her decision to interest Sophie wholeheart-
edly in her daughter's education, and yet she was aware
of the fact that there was still something missing from
the other woman's life. Surely sex wasn't so important
that it could ruin a person's life to be without it? She
had never thought it to be so, and yet the way Sophie's
life was developing, seemingly of its own volition, that
was the way it looked. She was aware of the fact that
although committed totally to Emily's upbringing,
Sophie needed more in her life. A lover seemed to be
the only answer.

The decision made, the mental block she had been
under the last couple of days seemed to pass, and the
words now flowed. The local doctor seemed to be the
most convenient man to bring in as the lover, his knowledge of Gerald's problem making him the obvious
choice.

It was almost three in the morning when Juliet got
this idea sufficiently on paper. It needed tightening up
in places, but she was pleased with the way it was shap-
ing up, going to bed with an easier mind.

Despite how late she had gone to bed she was up at
nine the next morning, remembering Jake's comment
about being here nice and early. She was determined
not to be at a disadvantage this morning; her hair was
neatly brushed, her light make-up faultless, her navy
blue fitted trousers and casual top giving her a look of

cool elegance when she went to answer the doorbell at nine-thirty.

'I know you said bright and early, but—Ben!' she groaned her dismay, her heart sinking.

'The one and only,' he grinned, walking inside without being invited to do so. 'Your newspaper.' He held it out to her.

The caretaker always put her newspaper on the door-step, but this morning she hadn't got around to picking it up. 'But what are you doing here?' she demanded as he made himself comfortable in one of the armchairs.

'Stephen said you weren't feeling too good last night, that you mentioned something about going out for the day. I'm here to offer to be your escort.'

'It's very nice of you to worry about my welfare, but I don't need an escort,' she said waspishly. 'I——' she broke off as the doorbell rang for the second time this morning.

Ben's eyebrows rose. 'Early visitor.'

'No earlier than you,' she snapped. 'Ben, you have to go. I——' The doorbell rang once again. 'Oh, damn!' She marched angrily over to the door, a feeling of in-evitability washing over her as she opened it and saw Jake Matthews standing outside.

'Good morning, darling,' once again he used the endearment. 'You look beautiful, as usual,' he murmured, pulling her into his arms and kissing her firmly on the mouth.

'Juliet, who—Oh.'

Jake raised his head to look at Ben with narrowed eyes, although his arms remained possessively about Juliet's waist. 'I didn't know you already had company.' He looked down at her with steely eyes.

'Ben was just going. Weren't you, Ben?' She gave him a look of pleading desperation.

'Was I? Oh—Yes, I was,' he agreed hastily at Juliet's warning look. 'Nice to have met you, Matthews,' he said as he went out of the door, a mischievous look in his eyes.

'Sheffield,' Jake gave an abrupt nod of acknowledgment.

'I'll call you, Juliet,' Ben promised as he closed the door.

The air was thick with tension once he had gone. Juliet extricated herself from Jake's arms, straightening her hair selfconsciously. 'I—er—Come in,' she invited, knowing that once again Jake had gained the wrong impression. It was perfectly obvious what he thought of Ben being here.

She could feel his anger as he followed her into the lounge, unwillingly remembering how ruggedly attractive he looked this morning, casually dressed in brown trousers and tan-coloured shirt, the latter unbuttoned partway down his chest, a dark smattering of hair visible there, the sleeves turned back to just below his elbows, once again the plain gold watch the only thing remotely resembling jewellery. If there was one thing she hated it was to see a man wearing necklaces and bracelets, especially the chunky kind that had been in fashion several years ago.

He made no effort to sit down, even though she had invited him to. 'When I asked if you had a date for today I should have asked whether or not your date of last night was going to run through to this morning,' he said contemptuously.

Juliet gave an impatient sigh. 'If we're going to have that conversation again . . .'

'We aren't,' he said grimly. 'But I thought it was Stephen you were seeing last night?'

'It was. Look, Ben only arrived about two minutes before you did,' she explained softly.

His narrow-eyed gaze searched her composed features. 'Is that the truth?' he asked.

'Yes, it is,' she snapped. 'Believe me, if I'd slept with

Ben I wouldn't lie about it.'

'No, you'd enjoy seeing my guts twist in agony,' he rasped.

'Jake!' she gasped.

'Wouldn't you?' he challenged.

She shook her head dazedly. 'I have no idea what you're talking about.'

'Oh, you know,' he growled, moving dangerously close, holding her in front of him with just the look in his eyes. 'You know that every time I look at you I want you, it churns me up inside to let you see these other men.'

'*Let* me see them?' she repeated furiously. 'I can assure you that *you* don't let me do anything! I do what I want, when I want, and I don't ask anyone's permission—least of all yours. You have some nerve——'

'Beautiful,' he murmured, his gaze fixed on her mouth. 'Absolutely beautiful.'

'I don't——'

'I'm going to kiss you, Juliet,' he said throatily. 'And this time I'm not going to stop.'

'Jake——'

'Yes—Jake,' he pulled her up against him, moulding her curves to his. 'Make sure you remember that as I make love to you. My name is Jake. If you call me anything else, Ben or Stephen for example, I'm likely to throttle you,' he warned in a growl.

She glared up at him. 'If you make love to me now the only name I'll call you will be rapist!' She struggled against him. 'And I won't be saying it quietly. How will that look, Jake Matthews accused of rape?'

His mouth quirked with amusement. 'What makes you think it will be rape?'

Suddenly she found herself free, and his expression was mocking as she straightened her clothing. 'That's the only way you'll get me into bed with you,' she snapped.

'We'll see.'

'We damn well won't!' her eyes flashed like clear sherry. 'Unless I haven't made myself clear, Mr Matthews, I don't go in for affairs.'

'Who said I want an affair?' He quirked a mocking eyebrow.

'Well, you certainly don't have marriage in mind,' she scorned.

'I don't?'

'No,' she laughed tauntingly.

'Okay, so I'm not in love with you, and I don't intend marrying you, but does that mean we can't have fun together?'

Her mouth twisted. 'You idea of fun and mine may not coincide.'

'How about seeing if they do?'

'I'm sure——'

'No, you aren't,' he chuckled. 'You haven't even given me a chance.'

'Maybe I don't want to.'

'Of course you do,' he arrogantly dismissed all her objections. 'Now, are you ready to go out?'

'Out? Out where?'

'Where would you like to go? I'll take you anywhere you feel like going.'

A spark of mischief brightened her expression. 'Anywhere?'

'Yes, anywhere,' he nodded indulgently.

She thought for a moment. 'How about Cornwall?'

'Cornwall?' he echoed hollowly.

'Mmm,' she smiled. 'I have this craving for a real Cornish pasty. Well?' she challenged smugly. 'Can you take me there?'

'You don't think I can, do you?' he drawled.

'No,' she laughed.

'Never challenge me, Juliet,' he told her seriously. 'I always meet a challenge, and I usually win.'

Juliet still smiled. 'Not even you could get me to

Cornwall and back in one day.'

'Maybe not in a car, but in a plane, yes.'

'A plane?' She hadn't thought of that.

Jake was enjoying her surprise. 'I have a small jet. We can be there within the hour.'

Her shoulders slumped. 'I've suddenly changed my mind.'

'And I've just made mine up,' he said just as determinedly. 'You wanted to go to Cornwall, and that's where we're going.'

'But——'

'Don't argue with me, Juliet. You'll find I usually win those too,' he mocked.

'Not with me you won't——'

'With you too.' He took her by the arm, pushing her bag into her hand before dragging her forcefully to his car.

She had never flown in a private jet before, never known the comfort, the luxury to be found there, from the carpeted lounge area with a drink cabinet, to the plush bathroom. She had travelled first class to America earlier in the year, but even that couldn't compare with the luxury of Jake's private jet.

'Television must pay well,' she taunted as Jake helped her on board, piloting the plane himself.

'Not this well,' he smiled at her, his eyes crinkled at the corners. 'Have you ever heard of Matthews Computers?'

Juliet sat down in one of the seats while he clicked her seat-belt into place, his dark head coming dangerously close to her as he concentrated on the task, his hair thick and dark, tiny lines visible beside his nose and mouth this close to:

'Not that I can think of, no.' She felt suddenly breathless.

'It doesn't matter.' He stopped in the action of straightening, a hand on either arm of her seat, his face

only inches away from hers. 'You aren't afraid, are
you?'

It was a double-edged question, and Juliet's mouth
tightened at his mockery. 'Not in the least,' she assured
him lightly. 'I've flown before.'

'Have you?'

Again the question seemed to have two meanings, and
again she chose to ignore it. 'You were telling me about
Matthews Computers,' she reminded him primly. 'I take
it you have something to do with it.'

'I own it.' He shrugged. 'I'm not always going to
appeal to the public, and my views won't always coincide with what's needed, but Matthews Computers can
never be taken away from me, it's mine. And what's
mine I keep.'

'I watched the show last night, by the way,' she said
dryly.

'And?'

'I still wish he'd taken a swing at you,' she laughed.

He returned that smile. 'Bloodthirsty little witch,
aren't you?'

'Now *that* would have been fun,' she mocked.

'I'll bear it in mind,' he said dryly. 'Mm,' he studied
her for a moment, 'maybe I should take advantage of
the fact that you're strapped down.'

'Don't you dare!' she panicked.

He gave a husky laugh. 'I wouldn't. I like a woman
to give me her full response when I kiss her.'

Juliet looked away from the intimacy of his gaze. 'This
is all highly ridiculous, you know,' she said awkwardly.
'No one in their right mind flies to Cornwall for the day
just to have a Cornish pasty.'

'No one said I was in my right mind,' he grinned. 'I
don't think I have been since the moment I first saw
you. And lovers do ridiculous things—they're allowed
to.'

'We aren't lovers!' She flushed.

'No, but I live in hope.'

'It will be a cold day in hell——'

'Tut, tut, tut, Juliet,' Jake shook his head. 'Most un-ladylike!'

'If you wanted a lady maybe you should have chosen someone else,' she snapped.

He was suddenly serious. 'I want *you*, Juliet. And I'm going to do my damnedest to make you feel the same way.'

'I don't——'

'Let's just enjoy the day,' he interrupted softly. 'I don't think I've ever eaten a real Cornish pasty,' he added teasingly.

She couldn't help laughing; she found that she laughed a lot during the day. Jake was very good company, the two of them acting like a couple of tourists, enjoying their Cornish pasty and chips with a pint in a local pub.

'Onions!' Jake grimaced after the first bite. 'You didn't tell me it had onions in.'

Juliet looked up from her own food. 'Don't you like them?'

'I love them, but it isn't polite to eat onions before you kiss a woman.'

Her mouth quirked, and she felt totally relaxed for the first time in ages. It seemed like years since she had taken a day off like this, since she had just forgotten everything but enjoying herself. 'If you're talking about me,' she gave him a cheeky smile, 'then——'

'Of course I'm talking about you!'

'Then I've eaten onions too.'

'So you have,' he grinned, bending to kiss her lightly on the mouth. 'Mm, you're right, I didn't notice the onions at all.'

'Jake!' she looked about them selfconsciously. 'You don't do things like that in here.'

'I do.'

'No!' She pushed him away as he would have kissed her again. 'Behave yourself!'

'As long as you promise to let me kiss you later.'

She scowled. 'That's blackmail!'

'That's desperation,' he corrected huskily.

Juliet didn't answer him, but concentrated on her food. This man was very persistent—and the trouble was he was getting away with it. She didn't like having her life taken over in this way, it made her feel insecure, unsure of herself. Jake also had the power to make her feel totally feminine, as if he would take care of everything—if only she would let him. Well, she wouldn't let him! She was a woman independent of men and emotions, and that was the way she wanted it to stay.

It was after six when they got back to London, and the unaccustomed fresh air and sunshine had made her feel very tired.

She turned at her door. 'I had a lovely day——'

'It isn't over yet.' Jake took the door-key out of her hand, unlocking the door before gently pushing her inside. 'Go and and get changed, and I'll take you out to dinner.'

'I——'

'Must you argue about everything?' he sighed.

'No. But——'

'Then don't.' He turned her around and shoved her in the direction of her bedroom. 'Go and change. I'll glance through your manuscript while I'm waiting.'

'Manuscript . . .?' she delayed.

'You've finished changing it now, haven't you?'

'Well . . .'

'It doesn't matter if you haven't,' he shrugged. 'I'll look at it as it is. The content of the story doesn't really matter at this stage, it's the style of writing that's important.'

Juliet licked her lips nervously. 'The *style* of writing . . .?'

'Yes,' he nodded. 'Every writer has a style. The story you've written may not be too good, obviously not if it was rejected, but if your style is good you may be able to write another one that's accepted. I believe I can tell whether or not you have a talent for writing,' he added without conceit.

'It really doesn't matter——'

'I insist, Juliet. Now go and get it,' he ordered firmly.

She did so, reluctantly, having looked out one of the old thrillers she had written years ago. She had read it through yesterday and realised just how bad it was. If her style of writing as Caroline Miles was obvious in that shambles of a story then Jake was indeed an expert on authors.

'Thanks.' He took the manuscript and settled down into an armchair, concentrating on his reading to the exclusion of all else.

Juliet gave him an impatient look before going into her bedroom. Maybe it would be better if he did find out the truth, then perhaps he would leave her alone.

She didn't hear any outraged shrieks as she bathed and changed, donning a casual knee-length evening dress, its royal blue colour doing wonders for her hair and eyes. It was a completely straight dress, showing each slender curve of her body, with a belt of the same material tied about her waist. She looked cool and attractive, ready to face Jake if he should have realised she was Caroline Miles.

He looked calm enough when she joined him twenty minutes later, his eyes widening in appreciation as he took in her appearance.

'Well?' she asked as he made no move to speak.

'You look beautiful. You're one of the few women I know who can look like an enchanting child all day and turn into a sophisticated woman in the evening.'

Juliet frowned. 'I hope that was a compliment.'

He smiled. 'It was.'

'Oh. Although I wasn't inviting comment on my appearance.' She looked pointedly at the partly read manuscript he was holding. 'What did you think of that?'

He put it down on the side-table, standing up to stretch his long legs. 'It's absolute rubbish,' he said bluntly. 'But then you knew that, didn't you?'

Indignation welled up inside her, her eyes flashing. 'I thought you said you would be gentle in your criticism!'

'You didn't let me finish,' he chided softly.

'Go ahead,' she invited tautly. Thousands of people had bought *Mason's Heritage*, and from the letters Michael had received, they had liked it. She would rather accept their opinion than this man's.

'This story,' he indicated the manuscript, 'is so full of holes it—well, it isn't very good. You bring characters into the story and just as soon forget them. It's obvious from the beginning who's behind the arms deal——'

'It isn't!' she protested.

'Samuels, right?' He quirked one eyebrow questioningly.

'You read the end!' she accused.

'No, I didn't,' he slowly shook his head, smiling. 'Don't take it so much to heart, Juliet. I only said this story was rubbish. You have the potential to write, and to write well, you just need the right storyline. It's mainly men who write thrillers—and I'm not being chauvinistic,' he mocked. 'I think you should try something a little softer, maybe with a love-story involved.'

'Become another Victoria Holt, you mean?'

Jake shrugged. 'Maybe. I definitely think that's the direction you should go.'

'And get accused of plagiarism?' she taunted.

'I only said that's the direction you should go, I didn't say you had to copy one of her books,' he said dryly.

Juliet picked the manuscript up, putting it away in a

drawer. 'I doubt I'll ever write anything else, so it doesn't really matter,' she dismissed.

'Sour grapes?' he teased.

'Not at all,' she said stiffly. 'I just don't have the time to write that sort of thing.' Well, she wasn't lying, was she!

'Pity,' he shrugged.

'But didn't you say there are too many people who think they can write?' she reminded him with barely concealed sarcasm.

'With you there's a difference. I *know* you can write.'

'Really?' she scorned. 'Maybe you should go into publishing.'

'Maybe I should. I'm not going to get angry, Juliet,' he warned, 'so you might as well stop trying to annoy me.'

She turned away. 'And why should I want to anger you?'

'To get rid of me. Didn't you have fun today? The truth now, Juliet,' he taunted.

'Why should I lie?' She faced him. 'Of course I had fun, what girl wouldn't when you go to those lengths to please her?'

'Then why are you trying to force me out now?'

'I'm not——'

'You are. But I'm not going anywhere without you, so you can forget it. Now,' he said briskly, 'did I meet your challenge?'

'You know you did,' she muttered.

'Then give in gracefully about dinner. And I'm warning you, Juliet, any challenge you throw out at me I'll meet. And I'll keep on meeting them, until you give in. Now, let's go. I have to change too.'

His apartment wasn't quite what she had expected. Oh, it was masculinely furnished and decorated, but comfortably so, with scatter cushions on the floor and sofa, magazines and books lying casually about the room. And the kitchen had every modern convenience imaginable, immaculately clean, although Jake assured her he often cooked for himself.

'Make yourself at home,' he invited once they were in the lounge. 'I'll just shower and change. Help yourself to my library,' he indicated the rows of books that covered the whole of one wall.

She found a complete mixture of tastes, from thrillers and murders to the slightly supernatural. Only Westerns seemed to be missing, even the occasional romance being included in the collection. She was surprised to see *Mason's Heritage* among their number, and took it off the shelf to casually leaf through it. On almost every page something had been underlined in red ink, sometimes only a word, sometimes a whole paragraph.

She was frowning over it when Jake came back into the room, freshly showered, his hair still damp, wearing black trousers now, pulling a black shirt on over his muscular shoulders, beginning to button it as he walked over to join her at the bookcase.

'*Mason's Heritage.*' His mouth twisted. 'I thought you said you'd read it?' He tucked his shirt into his trousers, buttoning the cuffs.

'I have. Obviously so have you,' she looked pointedly at the red pen marks. 'Why did you do that?'

'I like to check into historical novels,' Jake dismissed.

'I see.' She closed the book with a snap. 'And did Miss Miles pass?'

'As far as the research goes, yes.'

'I'm sure she would be surprised to hear it. After the things you said about the book on your programme I'm sure she would like to hear there was something right about it.'

He took the book out of her hand, and put it back on the shelf. 'She can't have been that bothered by my criticism; Michael tells me she's writing a sequel.'

Juliet looked away. 'Really?'

'Yes,' he grinned. 'You can't imagine how I'm looking forward to reading it.'

Her mouth tightened. 'I *can* imagine.'

Jake wandered back into his bedroom to collect a light grey jacket, shrugging his shoulders into it. 'Let's go and eat. Your Cornish pasty might have been filling at the time, but I'm hungry again now.'

Surprisingly so was she, and she enjoyed the dinner he insisted on paying for. She had made a move to take the bill, always liking to pay her own way, and Jake had shown her a hardness of his nature that hadn't been evident all day.

'This may be the age of equality,' he snapped, firmly taking the bill out of her hand, 'but when I invite a woman out to dinner I don't expect her to pay for it.'

'But you paid for lunch——'

'And I'll pay for breakfast too if I invite you to share it with me.' His usually lazy blue eyes blazed.

'I wouldn't accept!' she bridled angrily.

'The breakfast or the invitation?' he drawled.

'Either!'

'Why are you always on the defensive, Juliet?' he mused. 'Don't you like to flirt with a man?'

'No.'

'But it's half the fun,' he chided.

'Is that all you ever think of, fun?' she flashed, her eyes sparkling angrily. 'I happen to think there's more to a relationship than flirting and having fun.'

'Like respect and liking?'

'Well, I—Yes,' she agreed agitatedly.

'But I do like and respect you.'

'You—I—Oh, I give up!' she sighed angrily. 'Can we go now, I'm very tired.'

Jake shook his head. 'You're out of condition. All that walking along the beach has worn you out.' He stood up, pulling her chair back for her. 'You don't get enough exercise,' he murmured close to her ear.

The look she shot at him spoke volumes. 'I get all the exercise I need, thank you,' she told him primly.

'God, those eyes!' he groaned as they left the restaurant. 'I think I'll dream about those eyes tonight—as I have since the night I met you. They really are beautiful.' He helped her into the car.

'If it's only my eyes you like . . .' She gave a snort of disgust.

Jake was sitting next to her now, and turned to smile at her. 'Would you like me to list the different parts of you I—like?'

'No.' She was glad of the darkness to hide her blushes.

He chuckled his enjoyment; her embarrassment had not escaped him. 'You're very refreshing, Juliet, one moment a sophisticate, the next a blushing child.'

'Of course I blushed,' she snapped. 'Your remark was very personal.'

'It wasn't, but it was going to be.'

She was glad when they got back to her flat, although she invited Jake in for coffee, just to prove she wasn't a 'blushing child'. How on earth could she be a child at twenty-four!

'Not tonight,' he refused smoothly.

To say she was surprised was an understatement. 'I— Well—Then thank you for today. I—I enjoyed it.'

'So did I. Can I see you tomorrow?' He turned in his seat to look at her.

'I have to work——'

'I didn't mean during the day. Tomorrow night, are you free?'

Neither Ben nor Stephen had made definite plans to see her, although she knew from experience that that didn't mean she wouldn't see one or both of them, as they often came round uninvited.

Jake put out a hand to gently touch her cheek, turning her face towards him. 'It's taking you a long time to decide whether or not you have a date tomorrow,' he drawled.

'As it happens, I don't,' she revealed reluctantly.

His dark brows rose. 'No Ben or Stephen?'

'Not so far, no.'

'Then come over to my apartment,' he invited.

'Your apartment?' she echoed sharply.

'Yes,' he grinned. 'I like to go out, but I like to relax at home sometimes too. I had the feeling you shared that like.'

'I do. But——'

'Then spend the evening with me tomorrow. I'll show you the rest of my library,' he added mockingly.

'Beats etchings,' she said dryly.

'Not too many women like books, not to actually spend an evening looking at them anyway, but I thought you might be different.'

Her eyes widened. 'You really mean it about looking at your books.'

'Of course.' He shrugged. 'I'm not above using bribery to get you in my clutches.' He gave her a lecherous leer.

'You're impossible!' she laughed. 'But I would like to get a better look at your library.' She had been so immersed in the markings in *Mason's Heritage* that she hadn't had a chance to look at the rest of his collection properly.

'I thought you might,' he drawled. 'You're a book-aholic like me, aren't you?'

'I do love books, yes,' she nodded.

'I thought so, by your own collection. We have a lot of the same tastes, you know.'

She shook her head. 'I don't think so.'

'But we do. Most of the books you have I have too.'

That did surprise her; she would have sworn they had nothing in common.

'We have the same taste in this too.' He tilted her chin before lightly claiming her lips, the kiss becoming more demanding as she made no effort to resist him.

It was just the same, that wild surging of pleasure, the same nerve-tingling excitement that she had thought never to feel with any man. Jake was kissing her as if he never wanted to stop, crushing her against his chest while his hands probed the hollows of her throat, the curve of her spine, all the time his mouth moving with hers in a kiss that became still more intimate, sending thrills of pleasure through her body.

Juliet's hands were beneath his jacket, her nails digging into his back as excitement spiralled out of control, her body trembling as Jake cupped one of her breasts through the soft material of her dress.

Jake drew back with a ragged sigh of satisfaction. 'If you were to invite me in now I'd say yes,' he said throatily, gently nibbling her earlobe.

Juliet wriggled out of his grasp, moving back to straighten her hair, looking anywhere but at him. 'Which is precisely the reason I'm not going to,' she told him abruptly.

'I thought you might say that.' He sat back in his seat, looking as dishevelled as she felt. 'But you'll come over tomorrow?'

'I——'

'Or I'll come to you, you take your choice.'

'I don't like being told what to do,' she snapped. 'I'm not sure I want to see anyone tomorrow.'

'But *I* want to see *you*. Which is it to be?'

Her mouth set angrily, as she realised that here was a determination stronger than her own. 'I'll come to you.' At least then she could leave when she wanted to, if he came to her there was no telling when he would go home. 'What time?'

'Seven. I'll get you dinner.'

'You really can cook?'

'I really can,' he chuckled.

'Tomorrow, then,' she said jerkily.

He nodded, bending to kiss her softly on the mouth.
'I'll look forward to it.'

'I'll bring the wine.'

His expression darkened. 'I'm not very impressed with
Women's Lib, Juliet,' he said dismissively. 'I like a man
to be a man, and a woman to be a woman, the more
womanly the better.'

'That's archaic!'

Jake shrugged. 'Maybe, but that's the way I am.'

'So no wine?'

'No wine,' he agreed.

As Juliet lay awake later that night she had the feeling
of being caught on a merry-go-round, with no way of
getting off it. And until Jake Matthews became bored
with her or accepted the fact that she really meant it
about not sleeping with him, she had the feeling the
merry-go-round wouldn't stop.

CHAPTER FIVE

WHEN the telephone rang mid-morning the next day Juliet instantly thought it was Jake. But of course it wouldn't be; he thought her to be at work this time of day. Well, she had been working, but typing *Mason's Fortune*.

It was Michael. 'How's the book going?' he asked cheerfully.

'Fine,' she answered cagily, knowing she had lapsed a little the last week.

'Think you'll make the deadline?'

'Probably.' She thought of the day four months hence that they had agreed on. 'Congratulations on the baby, by the way.'

'Changing the subject?' he asked shrewdly.

'Yes,' she admitted honestly.

'Okay. Yes, I'm pleased about the baby too. Although I'm a little worried about Melanie,' he added slowly.

'She isn't ill, is she?' she asked anxiously, instantly feeling guilty for not telephoning over the weekend to see how her friend was feeling. Something else she could blame on Jake Matthews; he seemed to have completely taken over her life.

'She isn't as well as she could be,' Michael told her. 'She keeps telling me that all expectant mothers feel that way, but I'm not sure . . .'

'Melanie's probably right,' she assured him. 'Most pregnant women feel awful for the first three months.'

'Yes,' he sighed. 'I was wondering if you could go round and see her this afternoon?'

'But of course,' Juliet instantly agreed. 'I want to have a chat with her anyway.'

'A womanly chat?'

'Maybe,' she hedged.

'And will Jake Matthews' name come up in this womanly chat?' he mocked.

'I doubt it,' she said haughtily.

'I'll bet!' Michael laughed, and rang off.

She made a short call to Melanie, arranging to visit her in the afternoon. She had to admit her friend didn't sound her usual bubbly self.

She didn't look it either; she was very pale and wan when Juliet arrived later that day, handing her the carnations she had stopped to buy on the way. 'To help cheer you up,' she explained. 'Michael says you're feeling down.'

'Thank you for the flowers, they're lovely.' Melanie rang for the housekeeper to put them in a vase. 'And it isn't me that's feeling down,' she said once they were alone. 'It's the baby. I've been violently sick all weekend.'

'Probably just a bug you've picked up,' Juliet dismissed, sitting opposite Melanie in the chintzy lounge. 'And nothing to do with the baby at all.'

'That's what the doctor said. I rang him this morning after Michael had gone to work, I didn't want to worry him any more than he already is. He said I could go in and see him if I wanted, but that he was sure it was going to pass.'

'There you are then, nothing to worry about.'

'I'm not so sure.' Melanie looked down at her still flat stomach. 'I have a feeling about this baby.'

'All new mums-to-be have "feelings",' Juliet teased.

'I know. But—Well, it just doesn't feel right.'

Juliet frowned, seeing her friend was really serious. 'If you're that worried why don't you go and see the doctor as he suggested? That's what he's there for, after all.'

Melanie pulled a face. 'I don't want to seem as if I'm fussing. One in the family is enough. Every couple of minutes or so Michael asks me how I'm feeling. It's very off-putting!'

'But sweet,' Juliet laughed.

'I suppose so,' her friend grimaced. 'So what have you been doing with yourself the last four days? Michael says you haven't been working on the book.'

'So he called you, did he?' said Juliet dryly.

'That's another thing,' Melanie sighed. 'If he has to go out for any length of time he keeps telephoning to see how I am.' She gave Juliet a teasing look. 'He said something about Jake Matthews . . .'

'Did he now?'

'Don't be mean, Juliet. Have you seen him again?'

'Yes,' she sighed, knowing she couldn't deceive Melanie.

'Oh, I'm so glad. Well, I think you're perfect for each other,' Melanie said at Juliet's scowling look.

'I hate to disillusion you, Melanie,' Juliet drawled, 'but the arrogant Mr Matthews doesn't have marriage in mind either.'

'I don't believe you,' her friend shook her head. 'Does this mean you've finished with Ben and Stephen?'

'No, it doesn't!'

'You can't mean Jake accepts your going out with them?'

'Yes,' Juliet said smugly, 'that's exactly what I mean.'

Melanie frowned. 'I wonder why,' she mused.

Juliet gave her a sharp look. 'What do you mean?'

'Well, it angered him so much when he found out about them that he stormed out, right?'

'Yes . . .'

'Then why has he accepted them now?'

'Because he knows he has no right to dictate who I see!' Although she remembered he had said something about her 'dropping' Ben and Stephen. So far he hadn't brought the subject up again.

'Maybe,' Melanie agreed, but she didn't sound very

convinced. 'So what did you do, go out for a romantic dinner somewhere?'

Juliet's mouth quirked. 'That came later.' She explained about Cornwall.

'You're mad!' Melanie gasped. 'The pair of you!'

'It was fun,' Juliet shrugged.

'It sounds it! And you're seeing him again tonight?'

'Mm,' she nodded.

'Then he isn't giving you much time to go out with Ben and Stephen, is he?' Melanie teased.

Juliet frowned. 'No . . . I don't suppose he is. Thank you, Melanie, I'm wise to him now.'

'Oh, damn,' Melanie cursed herself. 'Now I've ruined it for him. I—Oh dear!' she groaned. 'Excuse me,' and she stood up to rush from the room.

Juliet followed her, finding her in the bathroom being violently sick, tears streaming down her cheeks. 'It's all right, Melanie,' she soothed, wiping her brow with a damp flannel. 'You're all right now.'

Melanie turned to bury her face in Juliet's shoulder. 'You see how it is,' she choked. 'I just feel—*awful*!'

'I can see that.' Juliet held her friend as she trembled. 'I'm going to get you to bed and call the doctor.'

'Oh no——'

'Yes,' she said firmly. 'This can't go on. Come on,' she helped Melanie up the stairs and into bed, obtained the doctor's telephone number and called him straight away.

By the time she left the doctor had been out and diagnosed a severe gastric infection, confining Melanie to bed and giving her the allowable medication for a pregnant woman. Michael was with her when Juliet left, assuring her that he would take care of Melanie.

Stephen was standing on the doorstep when she arrived home, or rather he was propping himself up against her door, straightening as he saw her. 'I didn't think you would be too long,' he grinned.

'So you waited,' she said dryly, opening the door to admit them both. 'I have to go out, Stephen.' It was six-thirty already, which didn't give her much time to get washed and changed and over to Jake's at seven.

'That's okay,' he shrugged. 'I can't stay anyway. I just came over to see if we were still friends.'

'Of course we are. Do you mind if I go into the bedroom while we talk, otherwise I'll be late?'

'No, go ahead.' He settled himself in an armchair. 'Going out with Jake Matthews?' he called to her.

Juliet grimaced as she stripped off the sundress she had been wearing and went through to the bathroom. 'Do you and Ben have to tell each other everything?' she sighed, having a hasty wash before returning to her bedroom to don denims and a blouse. After all, they were only spending the evening at Jake's flat, there was no reason for her to dress up.

'Not everything, no,' she could hear the smile in Stephen's voice. 'We just——' The telephone began ringing. 'I'll get it,' he called.

'No——' By the time she had finished buttoning her green blouse and run out to the lounge it was too late, and Stephen was already talking on the telephone.

'It's for you.' He held out the receiver to her.

'Well, of course it's for me, I live here!' She snatched the receiver from him.

'It's Jake Matthews,' he told her softly.

She knew that, had known the moment Stephen said he was going to answer the call. 'Yes?' she said breathlessly into the receiver, shooting Stephen a furious look.

'Can you make it seven-thirty?' Jake said without preliminary, his voice cold. 'Something's come up at the studio. I'm sorry it's such short notice, but I've been ringing you all afternoon.'

'I've been out——'

'So I gathered,' he interrupted curtly. 'Is seven-thirty okay?'

What made Marge burn the toast and miss her favorite soap opera?

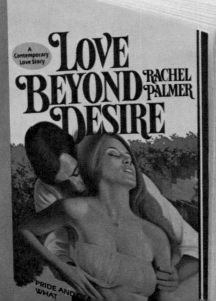

A Contemporary Love Story

LOVE BEYOND DESIRE

RACHEL PALMER

...At his touch, her body felt a familiar wild stirring, but she struggled to resist it. This is not love, she thought bitterly.

PRIDE AND
WHAT

A SUPERROMANCE™
the great new romantic novel she never wanted to end.
And it can be yours
FREE!

She never wanted it to end.
And neither will you. From
the moment you begin...
Love Beyond Desire,
your **FREE** introduction
to the newest series of
bestseller romance novels,
SUPERROMANCES.

You'll be enthralled by this
powerful love story... from the
moment Robin meets the dark, handsome Carlos and
finds herself involved in the jealousies, bitterness and
secret passions of the Lopez family. Where her own
forbidden love threatens to shatter her life.

Your FREE *Love Beyond Desire* is only the
beginning. A subscription to **SUPERROMANCES** lets
you look forward to a long love affair. Month after month,
you'll receive four love stories of heroic dimension.
Novels that will involve you in spellbinding intrigue,
forbidden love and fiery passions.

You'll begin this series of sensuous, exciting
contemporary novels... written by some of the top
romance novelists of the day... with four each month.

And this big value... each novel, almost 400
pages of compelling reading... is yours for only $2.50 a
book. Hours of entertainment for so little. Far less than
a first-run movie or Pay-TV. Newly published novels,
with beautifully illustrated covers, filled with page after
page of delicious escape into a world of romantic
love... delivered right to your home.

A compelling love story of mystery and intrigue... conflicts and jealousies... and a forbidden love that threatens to shatter the lives of all involved with the aristocratic Lopez family.

┌─ **Mail this card today for your FREE gifts.**

TAKE THIS BOOK
AND TOTE BAG FREE!

Mail to: **SUPERROMANCE**
649 Ontario Street, Stratford Ontario N5A 6W2

YES, please send me FREE and without any obligation, my **SUPERROMANCE** novel, *Love Beyond Desire*. If you do not hear from me after I have examined my FREE book, please send me the 4 new **SUPERROMANCE** books every month as soon as they come off the press. I understand that I will be billed only $2.50 per book (total $10.00). There are no shipping and handling or any other hidden charges. There is no minimum number of books that I have to purchase. In fact, I may cancel this arrangement at any time. *Love Beyond Desire* and the tote bag are mine to keep as FREE gifts even if I do not buy any additional books.

334-CIS-YKBH

Name	(Please Print)

Address	Apt. No.

City

Province	Postal Code

Signature   (If under 18, parent or guardian must sign.)

SUPERROMANCE

**EXTRA BONUS
MAIL YOUR ORDER
TODAY AND GET A
FREE TOTE BAG
FROM SUPERROMANCE.**

Mail this card today for your FREE gifts.

'Er—yes.'

'Fine. I'll see you later.' He rang off.

He had been angry, coldly, furiously angry. And much as she hated to admit it, he was probably right to feel that way. Every time he called or saw her he seemed to find Ben or Stephen here.

'I've done it again, haven't I?' Stephen said ruefully.

'Done what?' she asked absently.

'Made you cross with me.'

She turned to give him a bright smile, replacing her own receiver. 'I'm not cross with you.' With herself perhaps, for allowing Jake's anger to bother her. He had known about Ben and Stephen for days now, he had no right to act the possessive lover. He had no right to act any sort of lover!

But she was aware of certain feelings of guilt on her part when she arrived at Jake's promptly at seven-thirty, ringing the doorbell with a confidence that denied those feelings.

He was as casually dressed as she was, his denims old and faded, resting low down on his hips, the short-sleeved light blue shirt casually unbuttoned down his chest almost to his waist.

'Come in,' he invited unsmilingly. 'I would have offered to pick you up, but I thought your independent nature wouldn't like that,' he drawled, following her through to the lounge; a delicious smell came from the kitchen.

'It wouldn't,' she confirmed. 'I don't see the point of a man coming to collect you when you only have to come straight back again.'

'Very practical,' he taunted, 'but not at all romantic.'

She shrugged dismissal, and moved restlessly about the room, unwilling to sit down, not sure if she was staying.

'Who was he, Juliet?' Jake asked suddenly, his eyes narrowed as he looked at her.

'He——?'

'The man who answered the telephone,' he rasped. 'God, when he answered the telephone I felt like strangling someone!' His hands clenched into fists at his sides, evidence that the violence was only barely contained even now. 'Who was he, Juliet?' he grasped her upper arms, shaking her roughly. 'Who?'

'It—I—Stephen!' she gasped between shakes, starting to feel dizzy from his rough treatment of her. 'It was Stephen,' she choked.

His face became an ugly mask. 'And you spent the afternoon with him!'

'No——'

'Didn't you?' He shook her again.

'No. I told you no!'

'You'd better not be lying to me or I'll——'

'You'll what?' Her head went back in challenge.

His eyes glittered dangerously, a pulse beating erratically in his rigid jaw. 'I'll *nothing*,' he groaned achingly. 'God, Juliet, why do you do this to me? Why?'

She frowned her puzzlement. 'I don't——'

'Juliet . . . !' His mouth came down savagely on hers, grinding his mouth down on hers, bruising her tender lips until he finally realized his brutality. 'What have I done?' He drew back, touching her mouth with trembling fingers. 'Juliet, I didn't mean – God, forgive me!'

'There's nothing to forgive.' She withdrew form him. 'I'd like to leave now, I hope you understand—'

'No, I don't! I don't understand at all.' He ran a hand through his already tousled hair. 'Why do you need these other men?' He spun her around to face him, flinching as he saw her stroking her bruised mouth with a finger. 'Since the first moment I saw you I haven't even looked at another women.'

'It's only been five days,' she scorned, looking at her mouth in her compact mirror. It felt much worse then she was sure it really was, nevertheless it was sore.

'Five days, five months, five years—what the hell does it matter how long it's been! I think about you all the time, even when I should be sleeping—and every time I talk to you I find you with yet another man!'

'It wasn't another man, it was Stephen!'

His eyes narrowed. 'Stephen who?'

'Blake,' she supplied with a frown.

'Stephen *Blake*?' Jake exploded. 'My God, the man's old enough to be your father!'

'Stephen Blake the son, not the father,' she said patiently.

'I didn't know he had a son.'

'Well, you know now,' Juliet snapped. 'I have to go,' she told him agitatedly. 'My coming here was a mistake. We should never have met again after that first night. You're all wrong for me.' She picked up her shoulder-bag ready to leave.

'No—don't go,' his hand was gentle on her arm. 'I said I was sorry——'

'And that makes everything all right, does it?' Her eyes flashed like sparkling red wine, her stance aggressive. 'You'd tried and convicted me before I even arrived here tonight, all on the basis of who answered the telephone——'

'He told me you were just dressing!' Jake ground out.

She gave an angry sigh. 'I was—to come here. I'd been visiting Melanie all afternoon. She's having a baby, and she isn't at all well, I had to get the doctor out to her. I didn't leave her until six-fifteen. Stephen happened to be waiting for me. Your call came at twenty to seven,' she reminded him impatiently. 'Unless Stephen is a very fast worker we didn't even have time to go to bed together!'

Jake put a hand up to his temple. 'I—You—What do I do now?' he groaned.

'You don't do anything,' she said dully. 'Although knowing how chauvinistic you are, maybe you should open the door for me,' she mocked.

'I—Hell, what's that awful smell?'

Juliet could smell it too, the smell of burning food! 'I think it was our dinner,' she said ruefully.

'Oh no!' he grimaced.

'Oh yes.' She hurried into the kitchen, pulling the grill pan out to gush black smoke all over the kitchen. She instantly pushed it back again, switching off the heat. 'What is it?'

'Two thick, juicy steaks.'

He looked so woebegone that Juliet started to giggle, and Jake's eyes widened incredulously as she burst out laughing. 'You look so funny,' she explained her mirth.

'Oh, I do, do I?' He took a threatening step towards her. 'You won't think it's so funny when I put a plate of eggs in front of you.'

'I happen to like eggs,' she grinned.

'Good.' He took the pan out of the grill and threw it in the sink, running cold water on to it. When the smoke cleared all that was left was a blackened pan and two shrivelled up pieces of meat. Jake grimaced. 'Because eggs are all I have in the fridge.'

Juliet put her bag down. 'I'll cook them—I wouldn't want you to burn them too.' Her eyes were full of mischief.

'Juliet,' Jake gently touched her cheek, 'I really am sorry.'

She avoided looking at him. 'So am I.'

'You?' he frowned. 'But you have nothing to be sorry for.'

'Don't I?' she sighed. 'I came here tonight ready to do battle, just angling for a fight. I could have explained about Stephen straight away, but I didn't, I waited for you to explode. I'm as much to blame for what happened just now as you are. Now,' she said briskly, 'let's get the eggs cooked.'

In the end they had a hilarious time preparing the fluffy omelettes. Jake made a special dressing to put on the salad. Their laughter increased their appetites, and no food remained on the table by the time they returned to the lounge to listen to some records, Jake sitting on the floor at Juliet's feet, his head resting against her knees.

She didn't know what was happening to her! She had had a chance, a very valid reason, for walking out of here tonight and never having to see Jake again, and she hadn't taken it. She didn't even know why she hadn't. Just as she didn't know why, at this very moment, she was having difficulty preventing herself from running her hands through the dark vitality of Jake's hair, liking the way it curled slightly over his collar and ears.

Suddenly he turned, looking up to see the hunger in her eyes, and reached up to pull her down on the floor beside him, bending over to gently move his mouth against hers.

Somehow his gentle kisses weren't enough; her senses clamoured for more, her hands going up about his neck to deepen the kiss, at last allowing herself the luxury of touching his hair, her fingertips massaging his scalp as their mouths continued to move together in a message of eroticism.

He felt weightless as he covered her body with his, lying between her parted thighs, their bodies moulded together. One of his hands ventured beneath her blouse, claiming one naked breast possessively, touching the aching nipple with sensitive fingertips.

Juliet arched against him, feeling the involuntary thrusting of his thighs, the spasmodic show of pleasure in the hardness of his body, knowing an ache deep within her body that she knew Jake could more than satisfy.

When he parted her blouse to bare her breasts to his searching lips she knew pleasure so acute she thought she would faint, and she held his head against her, the sucking motion on her nipple causing her to cry out her pleasure.

But she wanted to touch him too, hastily unbuttoning his shirt to slip it off his shoulders, his skin darkly bronzed in the lamplight, his muscles rippling beneath her hand, their bare torsos seeming to burn where they touched.

Juliet explored the muscled perfection of him, his broad shoulders, his chest covered with silky hair, following the path of that hair to his navel, then hesitated about going further, her hands fluttering against his taut stomach.

Jake gasped, shuddering against her, his tongue moving against her hardened nipple, holding her thighs against him, telling her of his desire for her, his need for complete possession.

His lips returned to hers, caressing, gentling, calming, lifting his head to rest against her breasts, breathing deeply. 'I feel like a teenager,' he murmured ruefully. 'It must be years since I tried to seduce a woman on the floor,' he added huskily.

Tried to seduce? He must know he had succeeded, that even now her body cried out for his. Then why had he stopped, why now, when she wanted him so much?

He looked up at her with darkened blue eyes. 'Am I hurting you?'

She knew he referred to his weight on her, and now that passion was slowly dying she had to admit he felt quite heavy. 'A little,' she nodded, evading his gaze.

'Sorry,' he grimaced, and moved off her to lever himself to his feet, watching her as she hastily buttoned her blouse, the taut nipples still visible against the silky material. 'I guess a hundred and seventy pounds is a lot of weight on a little thing like you,' he added lightly.

As she only weighed just over a hundred pounds herself, yes, it was. She too got to her feet, still puzzled as to why Jake had pulled back when he did. She wouldn't have stopped him, wouldn't have been able to, and yet he had had enough control to draw back even though she knew he had wanted her. Or maybe he just hadn't wanted her enough? Maybe——

'Juliet?' He came to stand just in front of her, curving her body to his, his desire still in evidence.

'Why——' she licked her lips nervously. 'Why didn't you——'

He kissed her lingeringly on the mouth. 'Because now isn't the right time for us,' he told her huskily.

'Not the right time?' She raised startled eyes. 'But that first night——'

'I had the wrong impression about you. God knows you've told me often enough that you don't sleep around.' He smiled. 'I don't want you hurling it in my face that I took advantage of you when your defences were down.'

'But——'

'Let's have some coffee, Juliet.' He moved away from her, pulling on his shirt to rebutton it. 'Talk some more. We don't know each other well enough yet to go to bed together.'

'I don't understand you,' she said dazedly.

'You will,' he smiled. 'Yes, you will.'

Their passion was almost forgotten as they talked long into the night, Jake telling her about his childhood with his middle-class parents and younger sister. Juliet felt as if he were baring his soul to her, just waiting for her to do the same. But she couldn't do that, she never talked of her childhood or her family, the pain of the past went too deep.

'Tomorrow?' he asked as she stood up to leave.

'I—No, not tomorrow,' she refused.

His eyes narrowed. 'Why not?'

Her head went back at his possessive manner. 'I have other friends besides you, Jake,' she told him in a chilling voice, remembering Melanie's comment this afternoon about not being given time to see Ben and Stephen. Also what had happened between them earlier tonight had frightened her a little. She had had no control, had been influenced completely by Jake, and if he hadn't stopped when he had . . .

'Ben and Stephen?' he rasped.

Juliet nodded. 'Plus Melanie and Michael. I have several other friends I see too.'

'Male friends?'

'Some of them, yes.' Her tone was distant. 'Don't try to own me, Jake, because it won't work.'

His eyes were icy blue. 'I've never liked to share,' he warned. 'And I don't intend to make you the exception.'

'I have the perfect answer to that,' she scorned. 'If we don't meet again——'

'But we will!' he ground out. 'I'm not letting you go, Juliet. I'm not ready for that yet.'

'Maybe I am.' Her hands clenched at her sides.

'No,' Jake shook his head. 'We'll see this through to the end.'

Her eyes flashed. 'You make it sound like a contest!'

'It is,' he nodded. 'You challenge me, and I have to face that challenge. So far we're even. Now how about Wednesday?'

'I——'

'Yes, Wednesday,' he overrode her objections. 'And this time we'll go out to dinner,' he added lightly. 'I don't want a repeat of tonight. Come on, I'll walk you down to your car.'

'There's no need——'

'I'm a chauvinist, remember?' he mocked.

Juliet gave in with good grace, knowing she would have to in the end anyway. Jake wasn't a man who took no for an answer.

As she lay in bed later that night she knew no man had ever affected her as deeply as Jake. She had been his for the taking, and her body still ached with a need that hadn't been fulfilled.

She called Melanie the next day, and could tell by her friend's happy tone that she felt a lot happier. The sickness was starting to fade.

'Although Michael's insisted I stay in bed today,' she moaned.

'The rest will do you good,' Juliet said unsympathetically.

'How's Jake?' Melanie asked slyly.

'Fine, the last time I saw him.'

'Which was when?'

'Last night,' she laughed. 'Really, Melanie, you didn't expect me to have stayed the night with him?'

'There's a thought!' Melanie giggled.

Poor Melanie, she didn't even seem to think it was a possibility. How little she knew! She hadn't been the one to withdraw last night, Jake had, and she still blushed every time she thought about it.

The book wasn't going well again. Having got Sophie into the situation of being torn between two men she had no idea what to do with her. She finally gave up in disgust, and gave herself an afternoon out at the shops.

The walk did her good, and she attacked the story of Sophie with new vigour, finishing the affair with the doctor when Gerald was killed in a riding accident, finding out a month later that she was to have the doctor's baby. The relationship between her other two children and their little half-brother would make an interesting concept to the story.

Juliet was aware that *Mason's Fortune* had much more sexual connotations than *Mason's Heritage*. Maybe because she was becoming more sexually aware herself?

No, of course not! She refused to accept that. Although the nagging thought of Jake's mouth against hers, his hands on her body, plagued her mind all evening, making it impossible for her to concentrate on anything, not her work, and certainly not the television she had switched on out of desperation.

She had started to doze off in the chair when the telephone rang. 'Yes?' She snatched up the receiver, shaking the blankets of sleep from her mind.

'Juliet? It's Michael——'

'Melanie!' She shot up in the chair from her lounging position. 'What's happened to Melanie?'

'She's losing the baby,' he choked.

'I'll be right over.' She was already standing up.

'We won't be here,' Michael told her hastily. 'The ambulance has just arrived, and I have to go.'

'Which hospital, Michael?' she managed to ask. 'Michael!'

He muttered the name of the hospital before ringing off.

Juliet didn't give herself time to think before snatching up her bag and car keys and rushing out of the flat.

If Melanie lost this baby . . .! God, if she lost it— Juliet didn't even want to think about it.

Michael was in the waiting-room when she arrived, almost tearing his hair out by the roots.

'What happened?' she asked anxiously.

'What a damn stupid—I'm sorry, Juliet,' he sighed. 'She got out of bed, felt dizzy, and fell over. One minute she was all right, the next, this,' he groaned.

'Melanie will be all right,' she assured him. 'She's young and healthy, she'll come through this.'

'But what about the baby?' he moaned, his face in his hands.

'Surely the baby isn't more important to you than Melanie?' she gasped.

'Don't be so damned stupid,' Michael snapped. 'Of

course it isn't. But it's important to Melanie.'

'Yes.' She knew he was right. 'Then let's just hope, hmm?'

'And pray,' he said grimly.

It was the early hours of the morning before the doctor finally came out to assure them that both Melanie and the baby were fine, that there had been some danger, but that Melanie was now all right.

'Can we see her?' Michael asked eagerly, the greyness starting to fade from his face now.

'For a few minutes only,' the doctor advised sternly. 'And just you, Mr Dickson, your wife is very tired.'

'Oh, but——'

'This is my wife's sister, doctor,' Michael invented. 'And she's come a long way. At least let her say a quick hello.'

The doctor's expression softened. 'Well, all right—but just for a moment,' he warned.

'You're an awful liar,' Juliet giggled as they went through to see Melanie, her humour all the more acute because of her relief over Melanie.

'Meet your new sister,' Michael said huskily to his pale but happy wife.

By the time they had explained the joke to Melanie they were all laughing, and Juliet was finally thrown out by a disapproving nurse, Michael joining her a few minutes later when he had said a loving goodnight to his wife.

'Thank you for being with me tonight,' he said huskily once they were outside in the car park, everywhere quiet and deserted—although that wasn't surprising, since it was almost three o'clock in the morning!

She squeezed his hand comfortingly. 'That's what friends are for.'

'Take tomorrow off,' he teased to ease the tension of the moment.

'Gee, thanks!' she laughed. 'You're so kind. I wonder

if you'll feel that way if I don't meet your deadline?'

'Probably not,' he grimaced. 'But I did appreciate your being with me.'

The traffic was still heavy, despite the lateness—or earliness—of the hour, and it took her some time to get home.

As she went to put her key in the lock the door swung open. Strange, she was sure she had locked it. Unless she had been in too much of a hurry? No, she was sure she had locked it, a reflex action. Burglars? Heavens, no!

She entered the flat quietly, looking about her warily, jumping nervously as a shadow detached itself from one of the armchairs, a hand reaching out to switch on the lamp, and Jake stood illuminated in its dim light.

CHAPTER SIX

JULIET gasped. 'What on earth are you doing here?'

'Waiting for you,' he revealed grimly. There was a dark growth of beard on his chin, his hair dishevelled, his clothes creased.

'But I—How did you get in?' she frowned, surer than ever that she had locked the door.

'I picked the lock,' he told her calmly.

'You picked—You broke in!' she accused heatedly, putting her bag down on the table.

'That's one way of putting it.' His mouth twisted.

'It's the way *I* would put it. How long have you been here?' she demanded to know, hardly able to believe the gall of this man. He had actually forced the lock to get into her flat!

Jake shrugged. 'Where have you been?' His eyes were narrowed.

'Out!'

'Where?'

'I don't have to tell you—You're hurting me!' she groaned as he came forward to twist her arm up behind her back, bringing his body close against her as he glared down at her.

'I'd like to do more than hurt you,' he ground out. 'I called you at ten o'clock, and when I received no answer I kept calling every half hour until one o'clock. Then I got worried,' he revealed harshly. 'All sorts of ideas ran through my mind, like maybe you were hurt and couldn't get to the phone to call for help. I even picked the lock because I thought that. And all the time you've been with some other man! Who have you been with, Juliet?'

'I——'

He increased the pressure on her arm. 'Who?' he demanded grimly.

'Michael,' she groaned. 'We——'

'Michael Dickson?' he said disbelievingly.

'Yes. But——

Jake thrust her away from him. 'You've been with your best friend's husband?' he rasped.

'Yes. You see——'

'I don't want to know!' He looked down at her contemptuously. 'That's the most disgusting thing I ever heard!'

'Jake——'

'Excuse me. I have to leave before I throw up!'

'Jake, listen to me!'

He spun round. 'I'm through listening to you,' he said savagely. 'It's bad enough that he's married, but to your best friend, a *pregnant* friend at that. You sicken me, you and Dickson both!' He slammed out of the flat, uncaring that it was almost four o'clock in the morning.

Juliet sank down weakly into the nearest chair, unable to take in what had just happened. Jake had to be the most savage person she had ever met—and she had the strangest feeling she was going to miss him.

She waited all the next day for him to telephone, if not to apologise then to at least ask her what had really happened. No call came from him. And she was too proud to ask Michael for Jake's number, even though she knew he must have it. Besides, she hadn't been the one in the wrong. How could Jake have possibly believed such things about her and Michael!

Melanie was in much better spirits. Tests showed that the fall had caused no permanent harm.

'I feel so silly now,' she told Juliet ruefully, propped up into a sitting position by three or four pillows.

'You shouldn't,' Juliet assured her. 'It's better to check with these things.' She had brought her friend some grapes and now sat beside her absently eating them.

Melanie eyed her curiously. 'Is there anything wrong?'

'Wrong?' she blinked. 'No, of course not.'

'Oh, only you've just polished off half my grapes.'

'Oh dear!' She put the bowl on the locker beside the bed. 'Sorry.'

'That's all right,' Melanie giggled. 'It must be love.'

'What must——? Oh no,' Juliet shook her head as she realised Melanie was talking about Jake. 'You couldn't be more wrong.'

'Couldn't I?' she quirked an eyebrow.

'No,' Juliet denied, not even feeling able to tell Melanie of the things Jake had accused her of last night. Melanie had enough on her mind at the moment, without being told that Jake believed her husband to be an adulterer.

'How is Jake?' asked Melanie.

'I wouldn't know,' she answered distantly.

'You two haven't argued again?' Melanie asked in exasperation.

'No, of course—Yes,' she sighed, 'we have. I seem to have done nothing but argue with everyone since we first met, and mainly with myself,' she added ruefully.

'Yourself?' her friend prompted gently.

'Yes. I know he's wrong for me, completely wrong, and yet . . .'

'And yet?'

'I keep right on seeing him, letting him bully me!' Juliet stood up to pace the room. 'I don't like it, and I don't particularly like him, but I keep right on seeing him!' She sounded angry with herself.

'I wonder why?' her friend mused teasingly.

'I have no idea,' she answered irritably. 'Oh, let's not talk about him any more. I'll only get annoyed all over again.'

'Okay,' Melanie accepted readily. 'They're letting me out of here tomorrow.'

'So soon? Oh, I didn't mean—I just——'

'I know what you meant,' Melanie giggled. 'But it was only a false alarm, there's no point in my taking up the bed.'

Whatever hang-ups Melanie had had about the health of this baby now seemed to have evaporated, and Juliet for one felt glad.

The book was going well now that she wasn't being bothered by Jake Matthews every moment of the day and night. She had managed to evade seeing Ben and Stephen too, concentrating solely on writing. The character of Emily was developing nicely, as was Charles, the clash between the young brother coming when Sophie died, and the question of inheritance arising.

She was well into the tussle between the three of them when the doorbell rang on Thursday evening. Damn, she could have done without the interruption right now.

She was even more displeased when she saw it was Jake. 'What do you want?' she asked coldly, keeping the door firmly closed against him.

He gave her a rueful look, tall and dark in close-fitting jeans and a loose-fitting navy blue sweat-shirt. 'To get down on my knees and apologise?'

'Don't be ridiculous!' She flushed her agitation.

'But that's what I do want——' He broke off as Juliet's next-door neighbour came out of her flat, giving Jake an appreciative glance before walking to the lift with an exaggerated sway of her hips. For all the notice Jake took of her she might as well have been a stick of furniture; his attention was all on Juliet. 'Would it be asking too much to come inside?' he asked patiently.

'Yes, it would!' she flashed. 'Now what do you want?'

He raised his eyebrows. 'Do you really want all your

neighbours to hear?'

'I couldn't give a—No,' she sighed her capitulation, opening the door. 'You'd better come in.'

'Thanks.' He didn't appear at all perturbed by her lack of enthusiasm.

Juliet moved to snatch her notebook up from the arm of the chair she had been sitting in. 'A letter,' she explained breathlessly, giving a hurried look around to make sure there was no other incriminating evidence lying around. Thank goodness she had had one of her rare purges of cleaning this afternoon! The place was spotlessly clean, all her notes and manuscript neatly locked away. She pushed the notebook into her desk drawer and ran her hands nervously down her denim-clad thighs, her tee-shirt straining across her breasts as she did so, showing every erotic outline with startling clarity.

The man facing her across the room was aware of everything about her, of her legs long and straight, the slenderness of her hips, almost boyishly so, her narrow waist, those oh-so-tempting breasts, the nipples taut and enticing, almost begging for his lips to claim them, to——

'Jake, I'm waiting,' she ground out.

'So am I!' He moved towards her almost as if in a daze. 'I feel as if I've been waiting for you for years.' He grasped her arms. 'Juliet . . .!'

'No!' She wrenched away from him. 'The challenge is over, Jake. You finished it on Tuesday night.'

'No!'

'Yes,' she glared at him. 'I don't want you here any more, messing up my life, judging me——'

'I know the truth, Juliet,' he cut in quietly.

'I—You do?' she frowned her puzzlement. 'How?'

'Melanie called me——'

'Oh, I don't believe it!' She gave an exasperated sigh. 'She really is the most interfering——'

'I don't think she realised what she'd told me,' Jake put in softly. 'She invited me over this evening for a drink——'

'A drink!' Juliet snorted her disgust.

Jake smiled. 'I suppose it was a rather feeble excuse, but I was desperate enough to take it. I was going mad not knowing how you were. And Melanie was only too glad to talk about you, just as I was only too glad to listen.'

He was trying to seduce her with words once again—and she wasn't going to be seduced! 'Go on,' she invited tightly.

He sighed. 'She was full of what a good friend you are, how close you've always been, how you rushed to the hospital on Tuesday night to be with her when they thought she might lose the baby.' He watched her closely as he said the last. 'How you didn't leave the hospital until you were sure she was all right, at almost three o'clock in the morning.'

Juliet was unyielding at the regret in his voice. 'All of which I could have told you myself—if you'd been willing to listen.'

'Which I wasn't,' he accepted. 'Look at it from my point of view,' he encouraged. 'I thought you were spending the night with Ben or Stephen, or both, and——'

'That's disgusting!' she flared, her body tensed for battle.

'So is the way you let them use you.'

'Use me?' she echoed in a chilled voice.

'Yes,' Jake rasped. 'Neither of them wants to marry you——'

'And I don't want to marry them either. But about one of them you're wrong—Ben does want to marry me.'

His eyes narrowed. 'He does?'

'Yes!'

'And your answer?'

'I'm still thinking about it,' she snapped.

'You can't marry him,' Jake ground out. 'Not when it's me you want.'

'You're damned arrogant!'

'I may be, but I'm also going crazy. I want you so badly I——'

'Want, want, want!' Her eyes glittered. 'I'm sick of hearing what you want. *I* want to be left alone!'

'No, you don't.'

'I do, damn you!'

'No,' he shook his head, and took her in his arms to gently kiss her on the mouth.

It was his gentleness that was her undoing, and she was melting against him within seconds, entwining her arms about his neck as she clung to him, returning the kiss with a fervour that soon made him forget all about gentleness, sweeping her along on a tide of passion so strong that surely it could only lead to full consummation.

Juliet wasn't even aware of being lowered to the floor, of the removal of her tee-shirt, of Jake's mouth against her heated flesh. It was only as she felt him undoing the button at the waist of her denims, felt the zip slowly lowering, that she realised what was happening, that this time Jake had no intention of stopping; his hand was even now on her hip, caressing and igniting fire as his hand lowered.

'No!' she gasped. 'Jake, no!' she pleaded as his hand tightened on her tender flesh, knowing he was fighting for control.

His face was buried in her throat, his breathing ragged. 'This is the second time in a week I've tried to seduce you on the floor,' he finally said ruefully.

Both of them knew that he hadn't tried at all, that he had succeeded! 'Maybe next time we should choose somewhere more appropriate.' Juliet attempted to lighten the situation.

'Will there be a next time?' He looked down at her with deep blue eyes.

'I think so, don't you?' she said huskily, knowing that whatever power this man had over her she couldn't fight it—certainly not at this moment, with Jake still stretched out so sensuously above her.

'I hope so.' He softly touched her cheek. 'I really am sorry about the other night. I was so damned jealous.'

'Yes.' She had known at the time what had prompted his anger, had known and hadn't cared, as long as it got his disturbing presence from her life.

'You're afraid, aren't you?' he said suddenly, frowning.

'Don't be ridi——'

'You are, Juliet,' he insisted firmly. 'You're afraid of caring for anyone.'

'I'm not!' Her eyes flashed and she pushed him off her, standing up to tidy her appearance. 'Just because I didn't run after the famous Jake Matthews——'

'Don't resort to insults, Juliet, they won't work.' He still lay on the floor, looking up at her. 'Did someone hurt you in the past, is that it?'

'No——'

'Don't lie to me,' he said gently. 'You've been hurt, I can tell that.'

She looked at him unflinchingly. 'You're wrong.'

'Am I?'

'Yes.'

'You've never been in love?'

'No.'

Jake frowned. 'Then what are you so frightened of? Why won't you let yourself care for me?' He stood up, and sat in an armchair, his gaze never leaving her face.

'I've only known you just over a week——'

'Time doesn't enter into it,' he shook his head. 'It took me about a minute to know what you meant to me.'

Juliet looked away. 'Men think with their bodies, not their minds,' she dismissed scathingly.

His mouth twisted. 'I'll admit that it was my body that was first attracted to you, but it didn't take my mind long to decide the same thing. You're beautiful, intelligent, and incredibly sexy. I'm surprised you weren't married long ago.'

'Not all women want marriage,' she snapped.

'Meaning you don't?'

'No!'

'The perfect woman,' he smiled.

'Not so perfect,' she taunted. 'I told you, I don't go in for affairs either.'

'So you did. I trust you don't intend that to apply all your life?'

'And if I do?'

'Then it's going to be a waste. You have too much to give, Juliet, to be alone all your life.'

'Chauvinism again,' she mocked.

Jake gave a rueful smile. 'Maybe. When can I see you again?'

'I——'

'I do intend seeing you again,' he interrupted firmly.

She gave in with a sigh, knowing he would only have to kiss her to get her to agree anyway. 'Not tomorrow?'

'I can't make tomorrow either.'

'Of course, your show,' she nodded. 'Who is it tomorrow?' she asked eagerly.

'James Franks.'

'Do you have something against interviewing women authors?' she flashed her resentment.

'No,' he shrugged, surprised at the question.

'Then why do you always have men on your show?'

'I don't.'

'You do,' she accused heatedly. 'The last five weeks you've had men.'

'That's because they've all had books out recently.'

'I can think of half a dozen women that have too—Catherine Cookson and Jackie Collins, to name only two.'

'Caroline Miles being a third,' Jake said dryly.

She flushed. 'Not at all. *Mason's Heritage* came out almost six months ago.'

'But maybe I should have her on to discuss the sequel?'

'Maybe,' Juliet evaded. 'I certainly think you're noticeably excluding women. And I'm sure it's mainly women who watch you,' she added bitchily.

Jake laughed. 'Jealous, darling?'

'Not in the least!'

'I was only teasing. I'm well aware of the fact that you don't have a possessive bone in your body.'

Didn't she? Lately she wasn't so sure about that.

Jake misunderstood her silence for assent. 'Whereas I am very possessive,' he added ruefully. 'Speaking of which, why can't you see me tomorrow? Are you seeing someone else?'

She smiled. 'Yes.'

'Who?' he demanded sharply.

'My mother.' She laughed at his stunned expression.

But he wasn't stunned for long, and got up to come towards her. 'You teasing little witch!' he accused threateningly, pulling her roughly against him to kiss her fiercely on the mouth. At last he raised his head, looking in satisfaction at Juliet acquiescent in his arms. 'You did that on purpose,' he chuckled.

'Even if it weren't my mother——'

He put firm fingertips over her lips. 'No more arguing, Juliet,' he said softly. 'I'd much rather be—friends, with you.'

She extricated herself from his arms with some difficulty, Jake unwilling to let her go, finally releasing her after giving her a brief kiss of possession. 'It's late,

Jake . . .' she said pointedly.

He nodded. 'And you have to get up for work in the morning. Which department do you work in, by the way? I rang the switchboard at Dickson Publishing when I was trying to reach you on Monday, but they didn't seem to have heard of you.'

It was a question she should have been expecting, and yet she hadn't, and she searched frantically about in her mind for an answer. 'Well, I'm only a very—er—junior secretary. I don't suppose they even know me on the switchboard.' Lord, how feeble! Surely she could have thought of something better than that! 'I don't even have my own extension,' she added.

'So Michael told me.'

She swallowed hard. 'Michael?'

'Mm, when I couldn't reach you I asked to be put through to Michael, and he said you had the afternoon off. That was when I tried your home.'

So Michael had kept her secret. That surprised her, but perhaps Melanie had persuaded him it was for the best.

'Shall we say Saturday, then?' Jake said briskly. 'I could call for you in the morning and we could spend the day together.'

Juliet shook her head, seeing his frown disappear as she explained that she would be seeing her mother off at the airport in the afternoon. 'And you know what it's like at airports,' she grimaced. 'I have no idea what time I'll be back.'

'How about if I come with you?'

'No! I mean—I don't think that's a good idea.' She gave him a strained smile. 'It will probably be boring. I'm only going to see my mother and aunt off.'

'I wouldn't be bored.'

'No, I—I really would rather go alone.' Her hands twisted together nervously. 'I could always meet you later.'

Jake's eyes were like chips of ice, his mouth a thin straight line. 'You just said you didn't know what time you'll be back,' he reminded her abruptly.

'No, but—well, I—I could always come to your apartment as soon as I get back.'

'Okay,' he agreed distantly. 'We'll go out to dinner when you arrive.'

'Fine.' She gave him a bright smile.

His goodnight kiss was as warm and passionate as his earlier ones, and yet Juliet knew he was displeased with her, that he was angry because she wouldn't allow him to accompany her to the airport.

How could she tell him, how could she possibly explain, that she had already had two stepfathers younger than Jake, and that she just couldn't take it if he should become the third!

Her mother was her usual beautiful self when she arrived the next evening, slim and petite, and at forty-four her hair needed no artificial aids to be kept the golden blonde it was.

The two of them were as different as chalk and cheese, her mother small and delicate, like a china doll, her features flawless, her eyes a clear artless blue, her taste in clothes impeccable, her hair shoulder-length and gently waving. She had the look of a fashion model rather than the mother of a twenty-four-year-old girl— and Juliet resented her for it.

'I've invited Aunt Josephine for dinner,' she told her mother stiltedly.

'Have you, dear?' her mother asked in a bored voice. 'That will be nice.'

It wasn't nice at all, she should have known it wouldn't be. Aunt Josephine was the exact opposite of her mother, tall and slender, with mousy brown hair, a pleasant rather than beautiful face, and a girlish excitement about even the simplest things. At forty she had never married, and Juliet had always thought that to be a pity, because she would have made a wonderful mother. Dared she admit that in the secret recesses of her mind she had even wished her aunt had been her own mother?

'Are you looking forward to your holiday, Aunt Josephine?' she made an effort at conversation.

'Very much,' her aunt nodded.

'You want to go to South Africa, do you?'

'I—Well, I—It will be very nice,' her aunt answered primly.

'Of course it will,' Juliet's mother put in sharply. 'We're going on a safari, you know, Juliet.'

No, she hadn't known. 'Isn't that a little ambitious, Mother?'

'Certainly not, it will be very exciting. Besides, our guide is a gorgeous man,' she added with a smile.

She should have known! 'Number Four, Mother?' Her voice was shrill.

'Don't be silly, Juliet,' her mother flushed. 'You know it isn't a year yet since Robert died.'

'I seem to remember you married Jim only ten months after Daddy died.' She looked at her mother with hard eyes.

'That was different,' her mother snapped.

'It certainly was.' Juliet stood up abruptly. 'Excuse me, I'll clear the table.' She carried the dirty plates out to the kitchen before she really lost her temper.

It was always the same, somehow she just couldn't hide her anger and hurt over the callous way her mother had remarried so soon after her father had died. Oh, she had known that her mother wasn't happy with her father—why else would she go away so often?—but the speed with which she had remarried, and to a man so much her junior, had only made her resentment towards her mother all the stronger.

'You shouldn't blame her so much, Juliet,' her Aunt

Josephine said quietly behind her.

Juliet spun round. 'Not blame her? She made my father's life a misery!'

Her aunt placed the used wine glasses on the work-top. 'Your mother wasn't happy either.'

'Then why did they stay together?' Juliet demanded fiercely.

Her aunt shrugged. 'They had you.'

'Me——? You aren't telling me that they stayed to-gether all that time because of me?' she scorned.

'Partly,' her aunt nodded. 'And because in their own way they loved each other.'

'Never!' she denied. 'How could my father love the woman who had made him so unhappy?'

Her aunt sighed. 'Stop looking at things so one-sidedly.'

Juliet breathed in angrily. 'And how do you stand it?' Her eyes glittered. 'The way she walks all over you!'

'She's my sister——'

'She's my mother, but that doesn't make me blind to her faults.' She grimaced. 'I live in dread of the next stepfather she presents me with.'

'Estelle is a very unhappy woman——'

'Maybe she deserves to be!' Juliet said vehemently.

Her aunt shook her head. 'You're too hard on her, you always have been. Estelle loved your father from the day she first met him.'

'And that's why she hardly waited for him to grow cold in his grave before she remarried!'

'Just because she loved your father it doesn't mean it all ends happily ever after. Your father had his faults too,' her aunt added quietly.

'If he did they were faults that *she* caused.'

'Juliet——'

'What on earth are the two of you doing out here?' cut in the shrill voice of Juliet's mother. 'Juliet, I've been trying to turn on your television set, but so far I haven't had much luck.'

Her aunt shot her a warning look, and Juliet controlled her temper with effort. 'I'll come and take a look at it.'

The 'fault' turned out to be the plug still lying on the carpet. 'Oh, you're so clever, Juliet,' her mother said in her little-girl voice.

She gave an impatient sigh. 'Don't try that helpless act on me, Mother. I know damn well you're as capable as I am, if not more so.'

Her mother looked at her with innocently wide blue eyes. 'Don't swear, dear. And why do you call me "Mother" in that way?—you always used to call me Mummy.'

Her mouth twisted. 'I'm a little old for that now.'

Her mother seemed to accept her explanation, quite happily watching the television while Juliet went to help her aunt with the washing-up. She gave a mental shrug, not really expecting any offer of help from her mother.

'Calm down,' her aunt chided.

'What?' She looked up from the sink of washing-up. 'Sorry,' she sighed as she realised she had snapped.

Her aunt smiled. 'I thought you were going to start smashing things.'

Her smile was rueful. 'I'm not that far gone. And I really am sorry about this evening, Aunt Josephine. You must be sick and tired of being involved in our squabbles.'

'I've always been involved,' her aunt shook her head. 'The two of you are all the family I have.'

'Poor Aunt Josephine!' Juliet gave a relaxed laugh. 'You weren't very lucky in your relatives.'

She felt more relaxed by the time they went back to the lounge, to see her mother curled up comfortably on the sofa, her attention all on the television.

She looked up as her sister and daughter entered the

room. 'All finished? You should have called me.'

Juliet ignored the remark, knowing she was supposed to. 'Anything good on television?'

'Not really, dear.'

She wanted to ask her mother why she was looking at it then, but she managed to bite her tongue. 'Anyone like a coffee?' she asked brightly.

'Thank you, Juliet,' her mother accepted vaguely.

'Not for me, love,' her aunt refused. 'I have to get home and finish packing.'

'Haven't you done that yet? Really, Josephine . . .'

Juliet closed her mind to the reprimand her mother was giving her aunt, and went through to the kitchen to get the coffee.

'I'm off now, love.' Her aunt joined her a few minutes later.

She kissed her warmly on the cheek. 'I'll see you tomorrow.'

Her mother was still on the sofa when she rejoined her, and handed over her cup of coffee.

'Thank you, dear,' she accepted absently. 'I always find this man so fascinating, don't you?'

Juliet knew before she looked at the television that it was going to be Jake looking back at her. Oh, he looked so handsome, so vitally attractive, the dark brown suit and cream shirt making his skin appear darker than it really was, the thick dark hair she had run her fingers through only last night brushed neatly into place. Once again he was handling the interview superbly, questioning the marine biologist with an expertise that spoke of a deep knowledge of the subject.

'He knows how to talk well,' she said grudgingly.

'Really, Juliet,' her mother gave a coy laugh. 'I'm sure I'm not interested in the way he *talks*!'

She turned on her mother angrily. 'All men are conquests to you, aren't they?' she snapped. 'Never mind their intelligence, it's the body that interests you——'

'Juliet!' her mother gasped, going pale. 'Juliet, you shouldn't talk that way. I only said——'

'I know what you said!' Juliet slammed her coffee cup down on the table. 'Well, you can keep your greedy little hands off Jake, because he's mine—*mine*, do you understand?'

'Yes, dear. But——'

'And stop calling me dear!' she shouted forcefully.

'Yes, de—er—Juliet. But do you mean to tell me that you and this man Jake Matthews are going out together?'

'And if we are?' she asked guardedly, realising that in her anger she might have said too much, revealed too much.

'Well, I think that's wonderful,' her mother sounded genuinely pleased. 'I'm so happy for you, darling. Ben and Stephen are nice men, but—well, Jake Matthews is something else. Have you been seeing him long?'

'Not long, no,' Juliet answered dully. She wasn't so much shocked at the way she had turned on her mother, that had happened before, too many times to count, but she had sounded so—so *possessive* about Jake.

She couldn't be falling in love with him, could she? No, of course she couldn't! She never intended to let herself fall in love with anyone. But Jake pleased her physically, and although she might have denied it all these years, there was a lot to be said for physical attraction, physical excitement.

'Juliet?' her mother once more gained her attention. 'I asked if it was serious.'

Of course it was serious! Jake had got under her skin, had become important in her life without her wanting him to. 'No, it isn't serious,' she answered calmly enough.

'I suppose it was your common interest that first drew you together?' Her mother sipped her coffee.

'Er—yes.'

'Is he going to invite you on to his show?'

'You know I don't get involved in that sort of thing, Mother,' she dismissed. Thank goodness the titles were going up on Jake's show! 'I think I'll go to bed now,' she said abruptly.

Her mother looked disappointed, but didn't push the subject. 'I may as well join you, I have a busy day ahead of me tomorrow. Now, I gave you the keys to the house, didn't I?' She picked up her handbag.

'Yes,' Juliet nodded. 'And I'll try and pop down some time while you're away to make sure everything is all right.'

'Thank you, de—Juliet,' she kissed her absently on the cheek, 'I would appreciate that.'

Juliet was having trouble sleeping. What was she going to do about Jake? The obvious answer seemed to be to have an affair with him, to get this fever out of her blood once and for all. But what if she didn't, what if she went right on wanting him? But she wouldn't—would she?

CHAPTER SEVEN

SHE wasn't altogether surprised when the doorbell rang just after twelve. Jake—it had to be Jake. She pulled on her robe and moved quietly to open the door. There was no sign of movement from her mother's room, so hopefully she hadn't heard the bell.

It was Jake, looking just as attractive as he had on the television, only more so, his sexual aura at once apparent to her tonight, probably because she had been thinking about him so intently.

'Hello,' she greeted huskily, opening the door wide for him to enter.

He quirked one dark eyebrow warily. 'No shouting and screaming because I got you out of bed?'

She shrugged. 'If you want me to I will——'

'No,' he laughed, putting his arm about her shoulders as they walked through to the lounge. 'I like you just the way you are.' He pulled her against him, kissing her slowly, savouring every moment of his lips against hers. 'Mm, you taste good,' he murmured close to her parted lips. 'Is your mouth better now?'

'Yes,' she nodded.

'I'm glad. Juliet——'

'Juliet, I thought I heard—Oh, I didn't realise you had a visitor.'

Juliet turned to see her mother framed in the bedroom doorway, the light behind her showing the perfection of her figure through the gauzy nightgown and négligé. Her mouth tightened, sure the pose was a deliberate one; the night attire her mother wore was the same blue of her eyes, making her look youthfully attractive.

Her mother looked pointedly at Juliet. 'Aren't you

going to introduce us, dear?' she asked huskily.

Juliet pulled out of his arms. 'Jake, my mother. Mother, you know who this is,' she introduced tightly.

'Of course.' She moved forward with a grace that came perfectly naturally. 'Mr Matthews, how nice to meet you.' She let her hand be taken into his much larger one. 'I was only saying to Juliet this evening what a fascinating man you must be.'

'Thank you, Mrs Chase——'

'Prentice, actually,' she gave a selfconscious laugh. 'But please call me Estelle.'

'I'd love to,' Jake grinned, finally letting go of her hand—rather belatedly, Juliet thought! 'Juliet didn't tell me she had such a beautiful mother.'

'And she didn't tell me she had such a handsome— friend, either.'

Juliet turned away, sickened by this whole meeting. If her mother wanted to attract Jake then she was succeed- ing—he was lapping up her compliments like an in- experienced schoolboy.

'Well, I suppose you two must have things to talk about,' her mother was saying now. 'I'll go back to my room. Nice to have met you, Jake.'

'And you, Estelle.'

' "And you, Estelle",' Juliet mimicked furiously when they were alone. 'Perhaps you'd rather I had been the one to go back to bed and left you and *Estelle* together?'

Jake frowned his puzzlement at her behaviour. 'What the hell are you talking about?'

'I'm talking about you and my mother, that's what I'm talking about!' she said fiercely.

'I spent a few minutes being polite to her and you think——'

'Polite!' she echoed shrilly. 'That wasn't being polite, that was being nauseating!'

'Juliet——'

'Get out of here!' she snapped. 'Just get out—and don't come back!'

He stood firm. 'I'm not going anywhere until I know what all this is about.'

'My mother——'

'Is a very attractive woman,' he confirmed. 'But hardly my type, not when I have a passion for fiery redheads, and one fiery redhead in particular.'

Some of her anger started to leave her. 'I—You do?' she asked resentfully.

'I do,' he nodded.

'And you don't find my mother—sexually attractive?' She looked at him challengingly.

'Not in the least.'

'She's very beautiful,' Juliet persisted.

He shrugged. 'If you like small clinging blondes—and I don't. God, Juliet, she's your mother, of course I was polite to her,' he was angry himself now. 'But I certainly wasn't *attracted* to her.'

'You wouldn't be the first younger man to want her,' she muttered.

Jake frowned and came forward to raise her chin, looking deeply into her eyes. 'Is this what all your reluctance to become involved is about?'

She gave him a startled look. 'I—What do you mean?'

'Did you once lose a boy-friend to your mother?'

She laughed her relief, at once relaxing. 'Heavens, no!'

'It wouldn't be the first time it's been known to happen,' Jake persisted, his expression intent.

'Well it didn't happen to me,' she said lightly. 'You're the first boy-friend I've ever introduced her to.'

'And that was reluctantly,' he said ruefully.

'There's only six years' difference in your ages!'

'So?' he raised his eyebrows.

'And she came out here in that blue négligé——'

'Was it blue?' he murmured against her lips.

'You know it was,' she giggled, squirming her pleasure as he ran his tongue along the edge of her parted lips.

'I had eyes only for slim legs peeping enticingly beneath a brown bathrobe.'

'Liar!' she laughed, feeling more lighthearted now that she knew Jake wasn't interested in her mother.

'But I did,' he murmured against her throat.

'Jake, stop that!' She jerked away from his mouth probing the delicate shell of her ear. 'Jake, my mother is in the bedroom!'

'Damn your mother!' he growled, once and for all dismissing any doubts she might have about his finding her mother attractive. 'If she weren't here . . .?'

'Yes,' she confirmed huskily.

'You pick the damnedest times!' he groaned. 'Still, there's always tomorrow.'

She laughed teasingly. 'I might have changed my mind by then.'

'You'd better not,' he warned. 'You're enough to drive a man to drink,' he muttered.

'You?'

'Yes—me,' he groaned. 'Am I even allowed to kiss you now?'

She nodded. 'When you've told me what you came here for.'

'This *is* what I came here for,' he murmured against her lips. 'As I was driving home from the studio tomorrow suddenly seemed a long time away.'

'I'm flattered.' Her hands rested on his chest as she looked at him.

His expression darkened. 'I'm not trying to flatter you. You see before you a desperate man.'

'You look it,' she giggled.

'You won't find it so funny when we're alone tomorrow.' He chuckled his satisfaction as she blushed.

'I can hardly wait,' he laughed.

'Neither can I,' Juliet admitted huskily.

'I'm not sure I can cope with this sudden turnabout! Are you sure you haven't fallen over and given yourself concussion or something?'

'Very sure,' she smiled.

'It's all a little sudden, isn't it?' he frowned.

Juliet shrugged, moving slightly away from him. 'Maybe I've decided it's easier to give in,' she said distantly.

'Easier?' he mocked.

'Nicer, then,' she admitted grudgingly.

'Nicer?'

'More pleasurable?' she said throatily.

'That's better,' he grinned. 'Juliet——'

She evaded his arms. 'I believe you were just leaving . . .'

Jake gave an impatient glance in the direction of her mother's bedroom. 'Yes, I suppose I was,' he agreed reluctantly.

'Do you still want to come to the airport with us tomorrow?' she offered generously.

'I would have liked to,' he refused. 'But I have some work to do now, and——'

'It doesn't matter,' she interrupted brightly. 'You——'

He put his fingertips gently over her lips. 'It matters. It isn't often you make a move to spend extra time with me, and don't think I don't appreciate the gesture, but this work is very important to me.'

She looked at him with raised eyebrows. 'You sound very secretive.'

'I don't mean to,' he smiled. 'It's just that I've had a—project on the simmer for about six months now, and I think it's just coming to the boil. If it comes off I'll be able to tell you about it tomorrow.'

'I'll look forward to it,' she said sincerely, sensing a bubbling excitement within him.

He frowned. 'It may mean I'll have to go away for a few days.'

Juliet bit back her disappointment. 'I see.'

'You could always come with me?'

She looked up at him searchingly, seeing he was perfectly serious. 'No, I don't think so,' she laughed. 'I haven't got to the stage yet of daring to go away with a man.'

'Sure?' He grimaced his own disappointment.

'Very sure,' she smiled. 'Now it really is very late, Jake . . .'

'Yes,' he sighed, taking a reluctant leave of her.

She was just about to go into her bedroom when her mother's door opened, and she at once stiffened defensively. 'I hope we didn't keep you awake,' she said distantly.

Her mother shook her head. 'I've been reading. I—er—I hope I haven't interrupted—anything?'

Her eyes narrowed. 'Anything?'

'Well, if Mr Matthews is used to sleeping here——'

'He isn't,' she cut in angrily.

She received a teasing look. 'Well, it was a little late just to be visiting, wasn't it?'

'Nevertheless,' she said tightly, 'that's exactly what Jake was doing.'

'Yes, dear.'

'He was, Mother!' Never mind that the 'visit' would have gone on all night if her mother hadn't been here!

'If you say so, Juliet. But you don't have to hide your relationship from me. After all, you're twenty-four, and if you want to sleep with a man——'

'I don't!' Her hands were clenched tightly at her sides. 'Just because you have the morals of an alley-cat——' she broke off as her mother's palm landed painfully against her cheek.

'Oh God!' her mother groaned. 'I'm sorry, Juliet. But you——'

'I'm not going to apologise,' Juliet said tightly, refusing to show how shocked she was. Her mother had never hit her before, not even when she had been naughty as a child.

Her mother sighed, very pale, suddenly looking all of her forty-four years. 'No, I don't suppose you are. Goodnight, Juliet,' and she went back into the bedroom, closing the door firmly behind her.

God, what had she done now! She often argued with her mother, in fact they couldn't meet without arguing, but she could never remember attacking her mother in quite that way before.

It was impossible to sleep after such an ugly scene, and she was heavy-eyed and lethargic when her mother joined her at the breakfast-table the next morning, apparently suffering no ill-effects herself, but looking fresh and attractive in a light cotton suit and blouse.

'You look very nice, Mother,' Juliet offered by way of an olive-branch.

Her mother gave a grave smile. 'Thank you, dear. You look a little pale, aren't you feeling well?'

'I feel—I'm all right,' she said more calmly. 'Are you excited about your holiday?'

Her mother sighed, carefully replacing her coffee-cup in its saucer. 'Polite conversation isn't going to get us anywhere, Juliet. I think we need to talk, to talk properly.'

'We do talk——'

'Not properly,' Estelle shook her head. 'And it's long overdue. About seven years overdue,' she added dryly.

'Oh no, Mother,' Juliet stood up agitatedly, 'we aren't going to discuss Daddy.'

'We are.'

'No!'

'Yes,' her mother insisted firmly. 'I've let you keep him up on his pedestal at the cost of our own closeness.'

'We've never been close!' Juliet's eyes flashed.

'No, but we could have been.'

'Never!' she dismissed contemptuously. 'I've seen through you since I was ten years old.'

Her mother's mouth twisted. 'Then it's a pity you didn't see through your father too.'

'There was nothing to see through! He was good and kind, and what he ever saw in you I'll never know.'

'Oh, Juliet,' Estelle shook her head sadly, 'you're right, he was good and kind, when he wanted to be, but he was also fallible. We all are.'

'You certainly are!'

'And so are you,' her mother snapped angrily. 'You're so full of bitterness towards me you can't even think about things from my side.'

'I *saw* it, remember?' Juliet said bitterly. 'Ever since I can remember you went off and left Daddy and me——'

'And Josephine—don't forget Josephine.'

'I would rather have had my real mother!'

Her mother turned away. 'We can't always have what we want. I wanted all your father's love, but I couldn't have it.'

'You weren't jealous of me?' Juliet gasped.

'No, not of you.' Her mother looked at her with pained blue eyes.

Her mouth twisted. 'You aren't trying to tell me Daddy had another woman?' she scorned.

The pain flickered across her mother's face. 'That was only one of the things he did to humiliate me.'

'I don't believe you! He loved you——'

'Yes, in his way he loved me,' her mother nodded. 'But not as I wanted. And he loved this other woman too, for a time.'

'Until you brought him back to heel!'

'I pity you, Juliet.' Estelle looked at her sadly. 'And I pity Mr Matthews too.'

'Jake?' Juliet blinked her puzzlement. 'What does he

have to do with this?'

'He obviously cares for you. And you're incapable of caring for anyone.'

'That isn't true——'

'Yes, it is,' her mother shook her head. 'I'm afraid that between the two of us your father and I have destroyed all the love inside you.'

'Not Daddy,' she denied. 'Never Daddy.'

'It's never occurred to you that it might have been your father's behaviour that made me what I am?'

'Daddy's behaviour——? Oh, you mean this "other woman" business,' Juliet scorned. 'I don't believe you.'

'No, I can see you don't,' her mother sighed. 'Okay, we'll forget it. You obviously aren't ready to know the truth yet.'

'Not the truth as you see it, no.'

'Then maybe you should ask Josephine.'

'She knows about—this, too?' Juliet said hesitantly.

'Yes.'

'I don't believe——'

'Don't say you don't believe me again, Juliet! If you don't believe me then it can't do any harm to talk to your aunt, can it?'

'I—Maybe one day.'

'One day,' her mother echoed bitterly. 'And in the meantime I have to put up with your contempt.'

'You'll always have to put up with that,' Juliet snapped. 'If Daddy did have an affair then you must have driven him to it!'

Her mother put a hand up to her temple and stood up. 'There's no way I can win with you, Juliet. I accept defeat,' and she hastily left the room.

Could her mother really be telling the truth, could her father really have had an affair with another woman? It didn't seem possible of her sweet, gentle father. Her parents had been an odd couple, her tall, thin, bookish father and her petite, flighty mother.

Probably they should never have married each other—
but they had, and they had produced her! Thank
heavens she took after her father and not her mother.

It was a silent, strained journey to the airport; her
aunt seemed to sense the tension between mother and
daughter, and wisely remained silent.

Surprisingly there was no delay at the airport, and it
was only a little after four when Juliet got back to town,
much too early to go and see Jake, especially as he had
said he would be working. But she didn't particularly
want to be on her own, so she drove over to see
Melanie.

Her friend was in the process of crocheting a tiny
white cardigan. 'I'm sure it's going to be too big,' she
grimaced, putting it to one side.

'Not unless you intend having a midget,' Juliet said
dryly.

Melanie frowned. 'You think it's too small?'

'Well, babies aren't my speciality,' she teased, already
feeling in a better humour. 'But I would say it's just
right.'

'You think so?' her friend said eagerly.

She laughed. 'I'm sure of it. And how is the patient
today?'

'Very healthy,' Melanie admitted ruefully. 'Poor
Michael, I've been such a nuisance to him.'

'You were worried,' Juliet assured her. 'We all
were.'

Melanie pulled a face. 'I'm sure Michael isn't going
to believe me when the time comes to take me to the
hospital.'

Juliet laughed. 'He'll probably be panicking so much
he won't stop to question you.'

'I hope so. Anyway, that's enough about me, how are
you?'

'I'm well,' she answered noncommitally.

'And Jake?'

'Jake?' Juliet looked at her friend with innocently wide eyes.

'You're being mean again,' Melanie moaned. 'Are you and he back together?'

'Yes, we are, Little Mrs Matchmaker.'

'Me?' Melanie frowned. 'What did I do?'

'Ah, now that would be telling,' she smiled. 'But I'm grateful, anyway.'

'You are?' Melanie asked interestedly.

'I am,' she nodded.

'You—really like him, then?'

Juliet gave a deep sigh. 'I'm very much afraid I do.'

'Oh, that's wonderful!' Melanie gave a glowing smile.

'You won't say that when I come here to cry on your shoulder because it's over,' Juliet pointed out dryly.

'Maybe it won't be over.'

'It will,' Juliet said with certainty. 'Maybe not this month, perhaps not even the month after that, but it will be over. My mother told me this morning that I'm incapable of loving, and I think she's probably right.'

'Rubbish!' Melanie dismissed impatiently. 'Your mother has no idea what she's talking about.'

'Then how do you explain the fact that I've never fallen in love? All young girls experience calf-love, and unrequited love when they're older. I never have.'

'Not all girls go through those things,' her friend said stubbornly. 'Some women only fall in love once in their life——'

'Well, Jake isn't *it*!' Juliet scorned. 'I only said I like him, Melanie, this isn't the "grand passion".'

'You're so cynical——'

'I have to be,' she teased. 'Otherwise you would have the two of us married before either of us knew what had happened.'

'Oh you——!' Melanie gave her a disgruntled look.

It was seven-thirty by the time Juliet finally arrived at Jake's, dressed to go out to dinner in a thin wool-knit

dress in a rust colour that highlighted the colour of her
hair, deepening the sherry of her eyes. She looked coolly
beautiful, not at all like a girl who knew that tonight
she was to lose her virginity to a man who had her
physically infatuated.

Jake wasn't dressed to go out at all; his checked shirt
was unbuttoned to his waist, his denims creased. 'Hello,
darling,' he gave her a casual kiss on the mouth. 'Come
inside.' He preceded her, leaving it up to her to follow
him.

Juliet sat down, crossing one silky leg over the other,
showing a creamy expanse of thigh, but for all the notice
Jake took of her she might as well not even have been
in the room, let alone looking her sexiest, and wearing
the expensive French perfume her mother had given her
for Christmas last year. Jake paced the room restlessly,
occasionally glancing at the telephone, as if willing it to
ring.

'Is there anything wrong?' Juliet finally had to ask.

'What? Oh—no, nothing is wrong. I'm just waiting
for an important call.'

'I would never have guessed,' she said dryly, wondering what had happened to the impatient lover of the
night before.

'Sorry?' he looked at her vaguely. 'God, I'm being
lousy company,' he ran a hand through his already
tousled dark hair. 'Would you like a drink? Whisky?
Gin? I've got some wine . . .'

'No, thanks,' she refused.

Jake resumed his pacing, once more forgetting she
was here, still glowering at the telephone.

After another ten minutes of this Juliet stood up to
leave, smoothing the skirt of her dress down her thighs.

Jake looked at her with a frown. 'Where are you going?'

'Home,' she shrugged.

'Home?' He seemed to come out of his dream-world.
'Hey, look, I know I've been a bit preoccupied——'

'It isn't that,' she assured him with a smile. 'I'm not one of those women who have to be entertained twenty-four hours a day, I just don't think tonight was a good idea. You're obviously busy, and——' The telephone began ringing.

'My call!' Jake said eagerly. 'Don't go, Juliet,' he pleaded. 'This should only take a few minutes.'

She sat down while he took the call, trying not to listen, but finding it impossible not to.

'He has?' he said excitedly. 'That's great! When? Two hours? Of course I'll be there. Try and stop me!' he laughed. 'Fine, Frank, I'll leave straight away. 'Bye. Fantastic!' he murmured as he replaced the receiver.

Juliet was aware of only one thing, Jake was leaving, and right now. 'I may as well go,' she said dully. 'You have things to do . . .'

'Oh, darling, I'm sorry,' he sighed. 'I—It's just that this is so important. Broderick McCormick has agreed to an interview!' he announced disbelievingly.

Her eyes widened. 'Broderick McCormick!'

'Yes,' he said excitedly. 'Come into the bedroom and we can continue talking while I change.'

'Jake!'

'I'll be in the bathroom,' he taunted.

'Sorry,' she gave a rueful smile. 'I'm acting as if I've never seen a naked man before.'

He quirked one eyebrow. 'And have you?'

'No,' she gave an embarrassed laugh.

Jake put his arm about her shoulders. 'Come and talk to me anyway.'

In the end it wasn't as embarrassing as she had thought, Jake in the adjoining bathroom putting on a suit while she sat on his bed.

'How did you manage to get an interview with Broderick McCormick?' she wanted to know.

'Sheer hard work—and stubbornness,' he revealed with a laugh.

Jake was making light of it, but she knew it must indeed have taken a lot of hard work to get the famous author to agree to this interview. Broderick McCormick was a writer of continual bestsellers of sex and violence, intrigue, espionage, just blockbuster books about life as it was today. And yet he remained a recluse in his Swiss home, seeing no one and allowing no one to see him.

'But I have to actually leave now,' Jake said with regret. 'I've been trying to get the interview for months, and then yesterday he suddenly said he might be interested. I didn't dare mention it in case it didn't come off.' He came through from the bathroom, wearing a dark pin-striped suit now. 'You understand, don't you, Juliet?' he asked anxiously.

'Of course.' She stood up to straighten his tie. 'There, now you look perfect.'

'Wouldn't you know it!' he groaned. 'I now have you in my bedroom, and dare I say, willing——'

'You dare.' She gently touched the line of his jaw, her body curved against his.

'Willing . . .!' he murmured against her lips. 'Perhaps I won't go after all,' he muttered as his mouth claimed hers.

Juliet finally pulled reluctantly away from him. 'Yes, you will,' she laughed. 'I want to see the interview with Broderick McCormick as much as everyone else.'

'Then I'd better be on my way,' Jake grinned. 'Will you drive me to the airport?'

She straightened her hair almost shyly. 'Do you want me to?'

'I'd like you to come with me!'

'No,' she blushed. 'Not this time.'

'Does that mean——'

'Let's get you to the airport,' she said firmly.

There was something very impersonal about saying goodbye at an airport, especially to someone you didn't want to be parted from. Jake checked in, then pulled her to one side to say their goodbyes before he went through.

'I forgot to ask,' he frowned. 'Did your mother get off okay?'

'Yes.'

'Just—yes?' He quirked an eyebrow.

Juliet gave a rueful smile. 'We didn't part the best of friends.'

'Am I allowed to ask why?'

'No.'

'Subject closed?'

'Unless you want our own parting to be as stilted,' she said stiffly.

'I don't.' He pulled her into his arms regardless of the other people milling about the airport. 'I'm going to miss you, Juliet,' he murmured, kissing her lingeringly.

She was going to miss him too, more than she dared think about. 'Will you be gone long?' she asked huskily.

'Anything up to a week, I should think. If I'm not back by Friday they'll run one of the standby shows. And talking of my show, I've decided to take your advice,' he grinned down at her.

Juliet looked startled. '*My* advice? About what?'

'Female authors.'

She swallowed hard. 'You have?'

'Yes. I've asked Michael to arrange for Caroline Miles to come on the show.'

Juliet paled. 'I see.'

Jake seemed not to notice her distress. 'He wouldn't give me her address so that I could get in touch with her personally, but he seemed quite hopeful he'd be able to talk her round.'

'He—he did?' she gulped.

'Mm,' Jake nodded. 'He'd like the publicity for her next book. I have to go now, darling,' he said as his flight was called. 'Miss me, hmm?'

'I'll try,' she said jerkily, too disturbed by what he had just told her. 'You'd better go through, Jake. I—I wouldn't want you to miss your flight.'

'Neither would I, not now I've got this far. And I have the elusive Miss Miles to see when I get back. I'm looking forward to that.'

'Yes,' she said dully. 'You really must go, Jake,' she insisted as his flight was called for the last time.

He raised his eyebrows. 'If I didn't know better I'd say you were trying to get rid of me!'

'Oh no,' she instantly denied, blushing as she saw his look of satisfaction. 'I meant——'

'No, don't spoil it.' He gently touched her lips with his, drawing her into his arms to kiss her fiercely.

'Jake!' she gasped, stepping back, looking about them selfconsciously.

'I'll call you as soon as I get back,' he promised before striding away, tall and handsome, totally in command.

Juliet stood and watched him until he went out of sight, then turned away numbly. Michael had given Jake the impression that he would have her on the television show, which must mean that Michael wanted it too. She doubted she would be able to fight Michael, not when it was business involved.

And suddenly she no longer wanted Jake to know that *she* was Caroline Miles!

CHAPTER EIGHT

'YOU can't force me to do it,' she told Michael heatedly some minutes later.

She had driven straight to his home after leaving the airport, and confronted him in the lounge.

He shrugged. 'Did I say I was going to?'

'No, but—You told Jake you'd get me on his show,' she accused.

'I told him I'd try, I never made any promises.'

'You gave him enough encouragement to make him very hopeful!' she glared.

'Maybe I did——'

'You know you did! Michael, I won't——'

'Juliet,' Melanie cut in quietly, 'whether Michael did or didn't tell Jake he would get you on the show doesn't change the fact that you should have told Jake the truth by now, that you're Caroline Miles.'

'I—I couldn't,' she admitted reluctantly.

'Did you try?' her friend asked gently.

'I—No.'

'Then you have three weeks to do it,' Michael told her briskly.

'Three weeks . . .?' she gasped.

He nodded. 'That's when you're scheduled to go on the show.'

'I told you——'

'And I'm telling you,' he interrupted firmly. 'We need this publicity for *Mason's Fortune*. Heavens, no publisher in his right mind would pass up an opportunity like this for free publicity!'

'And how about the author?' she questioned bitterly. 'Don't I have a say in what I do?'

Michael shrugged. 'I think you've already had your say.'

'And had it dismissed!'

'Like you said, I can't force you to do it. No doubt *Mason's Fortune* will sell regardless.'

But he was disappointed in her, she could see that. And didn't he have a right to be? He had given her a chance, had confidence in her when no one else had. 'Michael, try and see it from my point of view——'

'I am trying,' he said grimly. 'And I think your behaviour concerning Jake has been totally juvenile——'

'Michael——'

'Let me finish, Melanie,' he requested softly. 'You should have told him from the first who you were,' he once again spoke to Juliet. 'By deceiving him you've not only put yourself in an embarrassing position but you've also put my company in an awkward one. I even had to cover for you myself once this week!' he added with disgust.

'The telephone call,' she realised dully.

'Yes,' he confirmed angrily. 'I didn't exactly lie to the man when I told him you were out of the office, but I didn't tell him the truth either. Now I want this situation righted, Juliet, because believe me, if he calls again and asks to speak to you I'll tell him exactly who you are.'

'Michael!' his wife gasped.

'He's right, Melanie,' Juliet sighed. 'I've known for days now that Jake has to be told the truth. But as for going on his show . . . I'm not sure about that. Give me a couple of days to think about it,' she asked Michael. 'Jake is away for a few days, so——'

'He is?' Michael asked interestedly.

'Yes, he is. So I have until he gets back to come to a decision.' She had every reason to suppose Jake would verbally rip her to pieces on his show when he found out about her deceit. That would be some debut on television!

'Where has he gone?' Michael wanted to know.

Jake hadn't told her not to talk about his interview with Broderick McCormick, and yet she had the feeling he had told her in confidence. 'He didn't say,' she evaded.

Michael gave her a look of disgust. 'I'll bet!'

She gave him a smug look from sherry-coloured eyes before turning to talk to Melanie. 'How is the baby coat coming along?'

Melanie grimaced, obviously relieved the argument between her husband and best friend was at an end. 'I'm doing a bootee now,' she held it up. 'It's smaller.'

Juliet laughed. 'You can't make him fifty pairs of bootees!'

'Him?' Michael questioned arrogantly.

'Melanie is convinced it's a boy,' she smiled.

'I hope not,' he grimaced. 'I can't stand the name Josiah. But you have to humour pregnant women,' he teased his wife.

'You have to humour *all* women,' Juliet told him softly, glad his anger had faded.

He burst out laughing. 'I don't stand a chance when the two of you gang up on me!'

Juliet had told Michael she would think about going on Jake's show, but over the next few days she did the opposite, pushing it to the back of her mind and concentrating on her writing to the exclusion of all else.

Emily was twenty years old now, very close to her half-brother Edward, less so to her older brother Charles, and was siding with Edward over the dividing of the estate on the death of their mother from a heart attack. Emily was also in love with James Harcourt, the local doctor, unaware of the fact that James was Edward's father. Juliet could just imagine Jake's reception to the sexual aspects of this book, she was rather surprised at them herself. But the book seemed to be writing itself. She just put the words down on paper. Where it was all going to end she had no idea!

Jake wasn't back for his programme on Friday, so one of his programmes from last year was repeated in his absence. It had been a good interview, and Juliet enjoyed watching him with the American author for a second time. It also gave her chance to look at Jake, to contemplate losing him. He would never forgive her trickery of him, he was too honest himself to understand her reasons—and she wasn't even sure of them herself now. The only thing she was sure of was losing Jake once he knew the truth.

On Saturday morning she decided, completely on the spur of the moment, to go to Devon and keep her promise to her mother to keep an eye on the house in her absence. She called round to Melanie to tell her of her decision so that she wouldn't worry if she should get no answer to her telephone calls; Melanie was apt to telephone her at least three or four times a week.

'Evading Jake?' her friend asked when told of her plans.

'Of course not,' she flushed. 'Why should you think that?'

'Well, he's sure to be back soon—from whatever mysterious place he's gone to. And you don't want to see him, right?'

'Right,' she confirmed with a sigh. 'I know I'll have to tell him the truth when he gets back, and I just can't do it yet.'

'You really like him, don't you.'

'I started out despising him, but yes, I really like him now. If he hadn't gone away we would probably be lovers by now,' Juliet admitted candidly.

'Instead of which that crazy plan you thought of a couple of weeks ago has become fact—you're going to surprise Jake on his show.'

'I must have been mad to think of it,' she groaned. 'Although fate seems to have taken the situation out of my hands.'

'Maybe it's for the best,' Melanie consoled. 'Honesty being the best policy and all that rubbish.'

'How you love your clichés!' Juliet laughed. 'Now tell me, how is the little mother-to-be?'

Melanie gave a glowing smile. 'I'm very well.'

The telephone was ringing when Juliet got back to her flat, and she sat down with a bump as she recognised Jake's voice.

'How are you, darling?' he asked huskily.

'I'm well,' she replied stiltedly, thrown in complete confusion at the unexpectedness of his call. 'And you?'

'Fine. I just thought I'd let you know that the interview went off well, and that I should be back early in the week.'

'That will be nice.' Oh, what was the matter with her! She wanted to tell him how much she was missing him, tell him to hurry home, and all she could say about his return was "that will be nice"!

'How has your week been?' he continued.

'Not too bad. I've kept busy,' she added with a nervous laugh.

'Have you been out much?'

'Been out . . .?' He meant with Ben and Stephen! 'I've had a quiet week,' she assured him, warmed by his jealousy.

Not that she hadn't seen Ben and Stephen, she had seen them both briefly, refusing their invitations to go out with them until she had worked out what was happening in her life. Neither of them had understood, but both of them had accepted her decision.

'And I've had a boring one,' Jake sighed. 'McCormick kept me cooling my heels for four days before he even agreed to speak to me. I'll be glad to get home.'

And she would be glad to have him home. It had been strangely lonely knowing that he definitely wasn't going to appear at her flat unexpectedly, even her work had not compensated as it usually did.

'Juliet?'

'I—er—Yes,' she licked her lips nervously, 'I'll see you when you get back.'

'Did you manage to miss me?'

'Now that would be telling,' she teased.

'So tell me,' he encouraged throatily.

Usually she found telephone conversations impersonal, and yet with Jake it didn't seem that way, his compelling warmth reached across the miles. 'All right,' she admitted huskily, 'I missed you.'

'That's all I wanted to hear,' he said with satisfaction. 'See you soon, darling.'

The drive to Devon was long and tiring, and it was late afternoon when Juliet arrived at the cottage she had been brought up in, memories seeming to crowd in on her as soon as she went inside.

It was typical of the cottages in this little fishing village, made from the grey stone common to the area, a thick thatch for a roof. And the inside was a credit to her mother's good taste, the character of the cottage preserved in the old-fashioned decor and furniture, the old stone fireplace big enough to walk inside. Upstairs there were three bedrooms, the white and pink one her parents had always shared, the lemon one her aunt had stayed in, and lastly her own little bedroom.

She was almost afraid to go into her room. She hadn't been home for years, not since she had walked out seven years ago, and she didn't know what to expect. Would her mother have changed it all, would her patchwork quilt have been replaced with a more modern one, would her pictures of pop-stars be taken down from the walls, her brush and comb and set of three different size cats removed from the dressing table? And would her collection of dolls have been packed away—or thrown away, the teddy-bear that had always lain on her pillow, even when she was seventeen, be removed?

She opened the door, slowly walking inside. It was all actly the same, everything as she had left it the day she had shouted at her mother that she was leaving home and never coming back. Everything had been kept lovingly in its place, dusted and ready, as if waiting for her to come home. And she never had!

She slowly sank to the floor and wept.

The next two days were a time of soul-searching for Juliet. She had always judged her mother from a child's point of view, had never stopped to question why her mother acted the way she did.

Well, she was asking now. Sadly there was no one to tell her the answers. Her mother claimed her father had had an affair, and yet she didn't see how that was possible. He never went anywhere but to the college in town ten miles away where he taught history. Could it possibly have been one of the female teachers there? It was possible; her mother didn't exactly have the sort of brain that could meet her father's on an intellectual level. Perhaps the affair had started out as a meeting of the minds and progressed to the physical? After all, her mother had been away a lot, and her father wouldn't be the first man to wander in the face of his wife's absence.

Most of the villagers remembered her, especially Mrs Wiggins in the local shop.

'I've read your book,' she gushed, 'and I did enjoy it.'

'Thank you, Mrs Wiggins.' Juliet handed over the

groceries she had collected.

'Your mother is so proud of you,' the shopkeeper continued to talk as she rang the purchases up on the till.

'Is she?' The question came without conscious thought, almost eagerly.

'Oh yes,' Mrs Wiggins confirmed, putting the groceries in a bag. 'She's so pleased with how well you've got on in London, the friends you've made. And she's so proud of how well your writing is going.'

Juliet blinked back the tears. Not once had her mother praised her writing, or the success it had given her. She had assumed it was because her mother didn't really consider it a career, her 'scribbling', she had always called it when Juliet was a child. And all the time she had been proud of her. It seemed the village people knew her mother better than she did. It was a disgusting admission to have to make about one's own mother.

'Don't be a stranger so long next time,' Mrs Wiggins smiled.

'I won't,' and she returned the smile warmly, paying for her groceries before leaving.

Later in the afternoon she went for a walk along the cove. The waves crashed against the high-sided rocks that protected this sandy cove, the water still and calm here, and several children swam in the clear blue depths, their laughter carrying in the wind.

Juliet stood up on the side of the cove looking down at their innocent enjoyment. She had often swum here herself as a child during the holidays from her London boarding-school, and just for a moment she allowed herself the luxury of wishing herself back to those carefree years, when she had been too young to know of her parents' unhappiness, when all life looked wonderful.

But reality came back all too suddenly, the screams from below no longer ones of laughter!

The mother of the young children was standing on the sea-edge screaming as one of the children drifted off on the air-bed she had been playing on, too terrified to get off it as she went out of her depth.

Juliet sprang into action, rushing down a hilly bank to the sand, throwing off her shoes.

'I can't swim! I can't swim!' the mother kept screaming at the top of her voice, tears of hysteria streaming down her cheeks.

Juliet almost shouted at her for the stupidity of bringing two young children, both of them under five, swimming, when she couldn't even swim herself.

The air-bed, with the petrified child screaming her fear, was nearing the opening to the sea, the current in the open sea strong and treacherous—if the little girl weren't pounded on the rocks before she could reach the open sea!

'Stay here, Juliet,' an authoritative voice suddenly ordered. 'I'll go.'

She swung round in time to see Jake shedding his shirt and denims, throwing them down on the sand beside his shoes before wading out into the sea, cutting through the water with strong strokes, reaching the child much quicker than she could ever have done.

After the initial shock of realising Jake was actually here, she could only watch in fascinated horror as he and the child went nearer and nearer to the gaping hole out to open sea, the jagged rocks taking on terrifying proportions in her mind. If Jake should hit those rocks, if he should——

He had the child in his arms now, the air-bed ignored, dashed against the rocks, sucked down by the force of water, never to be seen again.

Juliet turned away in numbed horror, knowing Jake was swimming back to shore now, the child safely on his back. It could so easily have been him that was crushed against the rocks never to be seen again. And if that had happened she wouldn't want to live herself. She loved Jake Matthews . . .

The little girl was being handed over to her mother now, both of them sobbing hysterically, the other child clinging to its mother's skirt in bewilderment.

'That isn't going to help,' Jake said sternly, instantly bringing a halt to the mother's crying. 'Get your daughter home, give her a hot bath and put her to bed for a couple of hours.' He pulled on his denims over his wet body, his navy blue underpants clinging wetly to his body, the denims doing the same once the water soaked into them.

The mother launched into a broken speech of thanks, collecting up both children ready to go home, assuring Jake she wouldn't let her children in the water again until she herself could swim.

Jake shook his head as he watched the mother and clinging children leave the beach, putting his arms in his shirt but making no effort to button it up, the cotton material already clinging to his damp skin.

Juliet looked at him with hungry eyes, devouring everything about him. She loved this man, had come to care for him without realising it. After all those years of contempt for love and the way it weakened you she still found it hard to accept the emotion into her life, to believe in it.

'All right, darling?' Jake came to her side, his eyes dark.

'If you hadn't come along——'

'You would have swum out there yourself,' he said grimly.

They walked up the beach together. 'How is it you're here?' she asked jerkily.

He shrugged. 'To see you—why else? I got back yesterday, and when you didn't answer your telephone all evening I rang Melanie. She told me you were down here. I left the car at your cottage and walked down to the beach.'

The cold wind ripped into them once they reached

the top of the cove, and Juliet felt sure Jake must be freezing cold, as they hurried the short distance back to the cottage.

Jake looked big and out of place in the cottage, his head almost touching the ceiling, his dark hair almost dry now, his shirt and denims still clinging to him.

'You'd better get them off,' Juliet advised, unable to look at him any more, her love still too new and untrusted.

Dark eyebrows rose. 'Juliet Chase, I'm surprised at you,' he mocked.

Her mouth quirked unwillingly. 'None of Daddy's clothes will fit you, you're much—bigger than he was, but I think his bathrobe might go round you.'

'Are you saying I'm fat?'

'Muscular,' she corrected. He had the build of an athlete, wide-shouldered, powerfully built, whereas her father had been very thin.

'And you want me to take my clothes off?' he drawled.

'Yes—not here!' she cried as he slipped off his shirt. 'Upstairs in the bathroom,' she told him hastily. 'Have a shower and I—I'll bring you the robe.'

Jake gave her a considering look. 'You haven't said hello yet.'

She gave a nervous laugh. 'There was hardly time for that.'

'There is now,' he invited huskily.

'I—You—You're all wet.'

'So?'

'So I'll get wet too!'

'Then you can come and have a shower with me,' he shrugged.

'Jake!'

'Come and kiss me, Juliet,' he groaned.

'I——'

'I've been thinking of you for the last week. Come

here, Juliet,' he repeated hardly.

She went to him as if in a dream, her arms up about his neck as their lips met in searing passion, uncaring of getting wet as she pressed herself against him.

Knowing it was love she felt heightened her senses, encouraging Jake to deepen the kiss by running the tip of her tongue along the edge of his bottom lip, instantly feeling the desire shudder through his body.

They were both shaking as they drew apart, Jake looking down at her for long timeless minutes.

'I think I'd better go and have that shower now,' he murmured at last. 'And I'd better make it a cold one!'

Juliet broke away from him, smoothing her hair self-consciously. 'I—I'll find you that robe.'

'You do that. And, Juliet . . .'

'Mm?' she blinked up at him.

'It's good to be home,' he said huskily.

'I—Yes. I'll show you where the bathroom is,' she said hastily.

Jake had to duck to avoid hitting the exposed beams when he reached the top of the stairs, as the ceilings on this floor were lower than downstairs. Juliet showed him the bathroom and gave him fresh towels before going to the trunk in the spare bedroom to find her father's old robe.

She had found these old clothes of her father's when she had explored the cottage, surprised once again by this streak of sentimentality in her mother. The clothes were apparently kept fresh and sweet-smelling, as if he too were expected home at any moment. Considering her mother had had two more husbands since it was surprising she kept such things; there were no visible signs of Jim and Robert ever being in her life.

She left the robe outside the bathroom door, then went downstairs to warm some soup through, putting a match to the logs in the fireplace. The cottage felt chill despite it being summer, but the logs soon caught alight, giving off a cheerful crackle as they flamed.

As she had known it would be, the robe was much too small for Jake, barely reaching his knees, the belt just holding the two sides together. He joined her in the kitchen, at once dwarfing the room.

'I—I made you some soup,' she said awkwardly. 'I thought it might keep off the chill.'

'Thanks.' He sat down at the kitchen table to drink the soup. 'A fire in August?' he mocked.

'I thought——'

'It might stop me getting a chill,' he finished dryly. 'Your thoughtfulness is to be commended.'

She blushed. 'How did your interview go?'

'All right, I suppose,' he grimaced. 'McCormick isn't an easy man to talk to.'

Juliet put a mug of tea down on the table in front of him. 'You won't look like that if you get a cold,' she snapped at his derisory glance.

'I suppose not.' He obediently sipped the tea.

'Do you think the little girl will be all right?' She sat down opposite him.

He nodded. 'She's just a little shocked. Her mother was in more of a state than she was. Let's hope it will have a lasting effect on her.'

Remembering the mother's white shocked face, Juliet thought it would. 'Would you like some dinner?'

'Are you offering?' he quirked an eyebrow.

'I—Yes.'

'Then go ahead. Will the car be all right parked out in the lane?'

She thought of the narrowness of the road and shook her head. 'I'd better move it.'

'I'll do it——'

'Not like that you won't,' she scorned his lack of clothing. 'Not unless you want to cause a minor sensation.'

Jake looked affronted. 'Only minor?'

'You're impossible!' she laughed. 'I'll put your clothes in the washer so that the sea water doesn't stain them, then I'll put your car in the driveway.'

'And dinner?'

'I can't do everything!'

'I'm hungry,' he grimaced.

Juliet thrust the biscuit tin in front of him, picking up his damp clothing to put it in the automatic washing machine. 'Your keys?' she held out a hand to him.

He gave her a mocking look. 'What would you say if I told you you've just put them in the washing machine?'

'Oh Lord, I haven't!' she panicked. 'Why didn't you say—You crook!' she accused as he pulled the car keys out of the robe pocket, jangling them in front of her nose.

Jake chuckled his enjoyment. 'Hurry up, woman, then I can have my dinner.'

She avoided his arms, snatching the keys from his hand, sticking her tongue out at him before going out to move the car. It was a lot bigger than her own, and the driveway wasn't all that wide. If she should smash into anything—But she wouldn't, she wouldn't give Jake that satisfaction.

She was just relocking the door when someone spoke from behind her, almost making her drop the keys in her surprise. It was the young mother.

'I just came to thank your husband,' she said shyly.

'Oh, but he——' Juliet thought of Jake wearing only the robe, and held her tongue. 'Would you like to come in?' she invited.

'I'm not disturbing you, am I?' The young woman followed her towards the house. 'Sharon's asleep, and my husband is at home taking care of Linda, and I didn't have time to thank your husband properly for what he did this afternoon——' She was obviously talking too much out of nervousness, and so Juliet let her talk. 'Mrs Wiggins told me where you were staying——'

'Mrs Wiggins did?' Juliet couldn't let that pass unquestioned.

'Oh yes. I described you to her and she told me you were staying at the Prentice cottage.'

'I see,' Juliet said tightly. 'Please come in.'

Jake was still sitting at the kitchen table when they entered, his gaze flickering questioningly from the young woman to Juliet.

'I hope I'm not disturbing you,' the woman blushed at his state of undress.

'Not at all,' he drawled, supremely confident. 'I hope you'll excuse my not getting up?'

'Of course. I was just telling your wife——'

'Wife?' he queried slowly, his eyes starting to glitter with revenge for Juliet's attempt to embarrass him.

The woman frowned. 'Mrs Chase——'

'Miss Chase,' he corrected. 'And my name is Matthews.'

Juliet blushed fiery red, sensing rather than seeing the woman's puzzled look. She should have corrected her in the first place, should never have given Jake the chance to embarrass her like this. Her omission hadn't been made out of any attempt on her part to embarrass him—didn't he realise that things were less worldly in this sleepy little Devonshire village, that this woman was openly shocked at the thought of the two of them living together—even if that weren't true?

'Of course it is,' the woman suddenly exclaimed. 'You're on television, aren't you? I often watch your programme.'

Juliet had to stand by while the young mother oohed and aahed about the fact that her little Sharon had been rescued by a real live television star—as if he could be a real *dead* one, she thought bitchily.

At last the grateful woman felt she had said enough thank-yous, and made a gushing goodbye, probably rushing straight off to tell her friends and neighbours about the television star who was staying at the Prentice Cottage with his girl-friend. Between her and Mrs Wiggins it should have spread through the whole village in—oh, about half an hour at most.

CHAPTER NINE

'How could you do that?' Juliet stormed at Jake, her eyes blazing.

'Do what?' he taunted, smiling his enjoyment.

'I thought it was easier to let her think we were married—in the circumstances.'

'Circumstances——? Oh, you mean the robe. Don't be such a prude, Juliet. Besides, I could hardly sit about in wet clothing. I'm sure Mrs Hewitt understood that.

'And I'm sure she understood no such thing,' Juliet snapped. 'It will be all over the village by now.'

His mouth tightened. 'So it's your reputation you're thinking of?'

'No! I—Oh, what does it matter?' she dismissed disgustedly. 'I'll get dinner ready.'

Jake watched her agitated movements about the kitchen. 'Anything I can do?'

'Get dressed,' she scowled. 'But that isn't possible.'

He frowned. 'Does nakedness bother you?'

'No,' she snapped indignantly, 'of course it doesn't. I just—Maybe you could go and sit in the lounge?' Her agitation was increasing as her awareness of him deepened.

He stood up, shrugging. 'If my sitting here bothers you——'

'It doesn't,' her eyes flashed.

'Then why are you shouting?'

'I'm not—Will you just go,' she said wearily.

'Juliet——'

She shrugged off his hand on her shoulder. 'Do you want dinner or not?' she attempted lightness.

'I do.'

'Then go into the other room. It's a pity to waste the fire,' she added by way of explanation.

Her breath left her in a sigh as he went through to the lounge, and she sank slowly down on to a kitchen chair, the food forgotten for a moment. Why did loving someone have to be so painful? The limbo she had existed in for the last seven years was much easier to bear.

And Jake had given no indication that he cared as deeply for her. Oh, he wanted her, and she wanted him, and wasn't that after all the best way to treat this relationship? She loved Jake now, but that didn't mean it would be for ever; it seemed to her it rarely was. Permanent relationships such as marriage broke up as easily as transient ones in this day and age of accessible divorces. Jake was offering her an affair, an affair that could be beautiful while it lasted, her faith in Jake as a lover complete, and she would be a fool not to take him up on his offer.

Well, she wasn't going to be a fool, not this time. She would take what he had to give, and when it was over she would accept that too.

His clothes were dry now, and after ironing them she took them through to the lounge. Jake was sitting on the sofa reading the newspaper, glancing up as she held out the clothes to him. He put the newspapers down. 'Thanks,' he nodded. 'I'd better go and put them on, perhaps then you'll stop looking at me as if I'm some sort of sex-maniac.'

Juliet smiled, relaxed now, her decision made. 'You aren't a sex-maniac. Or if you are, I must be too,' she admitted with a blush.

Blue eyes narrowed. 'What's that supposed to mean?'

'What do you want it to mean?'

His frown deepened, then he shrugged. 'I'll go and get dressed. And then I'd better start looking for somewhere to sleep tonight. Is there a hotel or inn in the village?'

There was one, catering mainly for the holiday trade, but she had no intention of letting him sleep anywhere but here.

'You can stay here,' she told him huskily.

'I don't think so,' he shook his head.

'Yes,' she steadily met his gaze.

Uncertainty flickered in his eyes, his look was considering. 'Aren't you afraid of what the people in the village will say—even if I would be sleeping in the spare bedroom?'

'But you won't,' she told him softly.

'I won't what?' he frowned.

'Be sleeping in the spare bed.'

'I—won't . . .?' He seemed less sure of himself now.

'No.'

'Juliet . . .?'

'Goodness, Jake,' she gave a nervous laugh, 'what does a girl have to do to get you to go to bed with her?'

His mouth quirked. 'Ask.'

She gulped. 'Ask . . .?'

'Is that so hard to do?'

'I—No,' she licked her suddenly dry lips. 'Jake, will you share my bed tonight?'

His breath left his body in a hiss. 'Will I ever know you?' he said wonderingly.

'Does that mean the answer is no?' It had never occurred to her that he would turn her down!

'Hell, no,' he laughed softly. 'It means the answer is yes. I just never thought—You're sure?' he sobered.

Juliet nodded. 'Very sure.'

He shook his head almost dazedly. 'A man could never be bored with you around, Juliet.'

'I hope not!' She gave him an impudent smile. 'Your dinner is ready, by the way.'

'Isn't it your practice to kiss a man after you've just propositioned him?' he teased.

'Of course.' She stood on tiptoe, kissing him lightly on the cheek. 'Enough?' she taunted.

'You know it isn't!' he growled, crushing her against him as his mouth claimed hers.

She was doing the right thing, she knew she was. Better to know a few weeks of this bliss than a lifetime of wondering. Better to feel love, to feel pain, for this short time. The wall around her emotions could be built again once her love for Jake was over.

Right now she didn't even want to think about the future, here and now the only thing that mattered. Jake's mouth and body were seducing her as they usually did, and her eyes were drugged with passion when he at last lifted his head.

'Let's go to bed,' he said huskily.

'Your dinner!' She instantly panicked.

'Can wait, surely?'

'I—No, I don't think it can,' she laughingly extricated herself. 'The pork chops will dry up,' she added nervously.

'Okay,' he shrugged. 'Give me five minutes.'

What was wrong with her? She loved Jake, she wanted him, and yet she had panicked the moment he mentioned going to bed.

It was just nerves, that was all it was. She would be better later tonight. Of course she would!

The dinner was cooked to perfection, although Juliet didn't eat much of it; she was too tense to relax. She drank a lot of wine to ease her nervousness, although Jake drank sparingly, seemingly already relaxed.

And why not? He had done this sort of thing many times before, it was nothing new to him. But it was new to her, and the coldbloodedness with which she had made the suggestion—and the cool way Jake was acting towards her now—made it all seem rather unpleasant.

'Shall we listen to some music?' he suggested after their meal.

'I—Yes, why not?' she agreed lightly, the wine having gone straight to her head.

She put on a rather loud Blondie record, turning it down slightly at Jake's wince. 'Would you like a drink?' she offered awkwardly.

'Scotch?'

'Of course,' she nodded, pouring a generous measure into two glasses, adding ginger to her own.

'So this is where you were brought up.' Jake looked about him appreciatively.

'Some of the time,' she nodded, sipping her drink, moving restlessly about the room.

'Some of the time?' he echoed.

'Boarding-school,' she supplied abruptly.

'You didn't like it,' he guessed.

Juliet shrugged. 'It was all right. But I would rather have stayed at home. My moth—my parents thought I would be better off at boarding-school.'

Jake didn't even show by the flicker of an eyelid that he knew she had meant to say her mother thought she would be better off. 'Where you met Melanie,' he said dryly.

'Yes,' she smiled naturally. 'She's been a good friend.'

He nodded, 'Is she all right now?'

'She seems to be, but you never can tell with these things. Apparently my mother seemed perfectly well until she gave birth, then the complications set in.'

'Complications?'

'Yes. But you don't want to hear all that,' she dismissed. 'Can I get you another drink?' she offered.

'No—thanks,' he refused slowly.

'You don't mind if I do?' she said merely for politeness' sake, already filling her glass.

'Not if you need one,' Jake said tautly.

'Need——? Of course I don't *need* one!' Juliet snapped. 'I'm just being sociable.'

'It isn't being sociable when you drink alone.' He put

down his own empty glass. 'You were telling me about your mother.'

'No, I wasn't,' she shook her head. 'You were asking me about her.'

'Well?' He rested his arm along the back of the sofa, turning to look at her.

'I wasn't an easy birth, and afterwards—afterwards, they told her she couldn't have any more children.' Juliet's mouth twisted. 'I don't think she even wanted me.'

'Did you ever ask her?'

She gave a bitter laugh. 'I didn't need to. Sending a small girl off to boarding-school, especially when her own father is a teacher, isn't exactly a common occurrence in this village.'

'And so you felt rejected.'

'I *was* rejected!'

'In your estimation.'

'In *any* estimation,' she corrected angrily.

'What does your mother have to say on the subject?'

'My mother——? Why, nothing.' She looked away, evading Jake's probing eyes.

'Which means you've never asked her.'

'No,' she confirmed tautly. 'Now have you quite finished psychi—psycho—Have you quite finished?' she compromised. Her tongue didn't seem to be working as it should, and she was beginning to feel distinctly light-headed. Maybe she should have eaten dinner after all.

'Do you want me to stop?' he asked mildly.

'Of course I want you to stop!'

'Why?'

'Because—because—Because I'd rather not talk about my mother. Unless of course you have it in mind to be husband number four? I think you might have a Big White Hunter as competition, but maybe I can put in a good word for you.'

'What the hell are you talking about?' An angry flush

darkened Jake's cheeks.

'My mother assures me that her guide on this holiday is some man,' she went on as if Jake hadn't spoken, each word wounding her, sickening her. 'But after tonight I may be able to give you the same recommendation.'

Jake sprang angrily to his feet. 'Take care, Juliet,' he warned softly. 'I'll only take so many of your insults.'

Her eyes opened wide as she tried to focus. 'Is it insulting to tell when a man's a good lover?'

'No——'

'Then I'm sure my mother would like to know. You're just the right age for her,' she added scornfully. 'She likes them younger than her. Daddy was ten years older, maybe it's more exciting to have a younger man make love to you.'

'Maybe it is,' Jake agreed tightly, dangerously so.

'Maybe I should try it—Oh!' Juliet gasped as his fingers made painful contact with her cheek. 'What did you do that for?' her eyes filled with tears.

'Because what you're saying offends me,' he told her grimly, unrepentant as her cheek showed the marks of contact with his hand.

'I'm so sorry——'

'Do you want me to do it again?' he threatened in a menacing voice.

'No!' Her eyes were huge, the colour of sherry against her pale face.

'Then shut up,' he snapped, pacing the room with impatient strides. 'Have you listened to yourself tonight?' he turned on her angrily.

'Listened to myself?' She cradled her aching cheek.

'Yes,' he said tautly. 'The fact that you invited me to share your bed——'

'I've changed my mind,' she told him hastily.

He shook his head. 'No, you haven't. Because I changed my mind about accepting a couple of hours ago. Women don't usually have to get drunk to be able to go to bed with me.'

'Oh, I didn't——'

'Yes, you did,' Jake ground out. 'Look at you, you're absolutely stoned! And all at the thought of going to bed with a man.' His expression scorned her. 'You aren't a woman, Juliet, you're just a female trying to prove that you are. Your femininity, your capability to love has been locked away for so long you have no idea where to start.'

She stood up angrily. 'How dare you!' Her eyes flashed.

'Oh, I dare,' he said grimly. 'Because I was fool enough to think I could actually mean something to you. You scorn your mother, but at least she has the courage to love, you don't have the first idea.'

But she did, she loved *him*. Then why were they arguing?

'Jake——'

'Stay away from me, Juliet,' he snapped. 'The mood I'm in I could do you some physical harm. I think it would be as well if I slept at the inn after all.'

'But——'

'Maybe one day you'll grow up, maybe you'll even realise that your mother is just another lonely lady looking for someone to love her. And maybe when that day comes you'll stop being so damned patronising. You might even try loving her yourself,' he advised harshly.

'Jake . . .' The room was starting to spin, blackness fading in and out. 'Jake, I——' She fell to the floor in a dead faint.

She woke in the morning with a terrible headache, and got out of bed to pull the curtains against the strong sunlight streaming into her bedroom, then gasping as she realised she was naked.

And she didn't need two guesses how she had got this

way! Jake must have carried her upstairs to her bedroom and undressed her before putting her to bed.

Memories of last night flooded into her mind—the way she had asked Jake to go to bed with her, the way she had drunk too much, the way she had talked to him about her mother. She had never shown her bitterness to anyone like that before—and it had obviously disgusted Jake. The things he had said to her . . .!

Where was he now? Had he kept to his decision and gone to stay at the inn? Somehow she thought he had. And she couldn't blame him.

She buried her face in the pillow, knowing it was over between her and Jake, that she herself had finished it. She wasn't a very pleasant person, her bitterness controlled her life, and Jake knew that now.

The door opened, jerking her up in the bed, pulling the covers up to her chin as Jake came into the room.

'Coffee.' He held out the cup to her.

'I—Thanks.' She accepted it gratefully, looking up at him apprehensively.

'Don't worry,' his mouth twisted, 'I didn't slake my manly lusts on you while you were unconscious.'

'I didn't think you had!' she gasped her shock.

'Didn't you?' he said coldly.

'Certainly not,' she said indignantly. 'And I wasn't unconscious,' she flashed.

'Weren't you? You certainly looked that way to me.'

'I—You—To her shame she burst into tears, putting the coffee cup down on the side table to bury her face in her hands, her shoulders shaking with her sobs.

The bed dipped to one side as Jake sat down beside her, pulling her into his arms. 'That's it, Juliet,' he soothed. 'Cry it all out. I think it's overdue.'

This man knew her so well, knew that she never cried, that she had done so only twice during the last seven years, and both times during the last three days.

'I'm sorry.' She finally pulled away from him, wiping

her cheeks dry.

'So am I,' he said deeply. 'Last night——'

'Oh, don't apologise for anything you said,' she cut in jerkily. 'It was all true.'

'I know that.' Jake stood up. 'And I wasn't going to apologise for what I said to you. Those things needed to be said, I'm just sorry I was the one who had to say them.'

Juliet swallowed hard. 'I see.'

He sighed. 'I know you can't accept what I said yet, maybe you never will. But that would be a pity.'

'I—It would?' She blinked up at him.

'Yes. Because underneath all the bitterness is a beautiful woman fighting to get out. It will be too late for her soon, and that would be a waste.'

'Jake——'

'I'm leaving now, Juliet,' he told her softly. 'I wish things could have been different between us, but—well, they aren't. You have a lot of growing up to do, and it may already be too late. Why don't you give your mother a chance, talk to her, share with her? You might find you like her after all.'

'I—Will I see you again?' she said brokenly.

He shrugged. 'If you ever do grow up I would be glad to see you. I think we could have had something good together. So give me a call, hmm?'

And that was that, dismissed from his life as if she had never been. 'How will I know if I've grown up?' she asked shakily.

'You'll know. Goodbye, Juliet.'

'I—Goodbye. Jake!' she stopped him as he reached the bedroom door, blushing as he slowly turned. 'Goodbye,' she said softly.

He nodded abruptly, and then he was gone.

Juliet gave a wounded cry, but she knew that Jake wouldn't come back, that he would never be back, that it was all over between them.

She didn't get up that day, didn't even know when it was night or day for the next few days. She did a lot of crying, a lot of thinking, and by the third day after Jake's departure she was a little calmer.

He had been right to get out of her life. Her body and mind might be that of a woman, but her emotions were that of a seventeen-year-old, her father just dead, her mother blamed in her mind for that loss.

And when her mother had tried to talk to her two weeks ago she hadn't wanted to listen, perhaps hadn't wanted to know the truth. She still wasn't sure she was ready for that, but one day she would be.

She telephoned Michael the next day, calming his panicked cry of where was she. She had taken the telephone off the hook the last few days, not wanting to talk to anyone.

'I tried all day yesterday to talk to you,' Michael complained. 'All the telephonist could tell me was that there was no fault on the line.'

'There isn't. I just didn't feel like talking to anyone.'

'Have you been working?' he asked eagerly.

'Not at all,' she laughed at his grunt of disapproval.

'Why haven't you?' he growled.

' "Woman cannot live by work alone",' she misquoted.

'Woman won't live at all if she doesn't soon get writing! Thought any more about going on Matthews' show?' he changed the subject.

'No.'

'You would be a fool not to——'

'I haven't thought any more about it, Michael,' she interrupted calmly, 'because I don't need to. I'm not going to do it.'

'Not going to——? Juliet!'

'The answer is no, Michael. Perhaps you could let him know that?'

'Why don't you tell him?' he snapped. 'He's there with you, isn't he?'

'He was, but he isn't now.'

'Had an argument, have you?'

'No.' The way she and Jake had broken up could never be called an argument.

'Then why won't you do the show?' he groaned.

'Because I don't want to.'

'You don't want——? What the hell is going on, Juliet?'

'Nothing,' she smiled. 'And stop swearing. Oh, and while I'm on the telephone I think I should tell you I don't intend returning to London.'

'Not returning? But——'

'You're starting to sound like a parrot, Michael,' she taunted. 'And no, I'm not coming back to London.'

'You're having a holiday.'

'No, I'm staying here.'

'But you can't!'

'Why can't I?' she laughed.

'Well—Because—Why?' he sounded confused.

'Why not?'

'Don't be flippant,' Michael snapped. 'You always said you'd never go back to Devon.'

'I said a lot of things that would have been better left unsaid,' she told him sadly.

'You sound different, Juliet.'

'I hope so,' she said fervently.

'Are you ill?' He sounded anxious.

'No.'

'Then why——? Look, come and see Melanie and me before making any final decision about staying there.'

'I'm coming to pick some clothes up from my flat later in the week, so I'll call in. But you won't change my mind, Michael. And you'll let Jake know about the show, won't you?'

'Juliet——'

'Michael!'

'Okay,' he sighed. 'But I think you're a fool.'

She knew she wasn't, knew that she still had a lot of growing up to do before she saw Jake again. And she was determined she would see him again.

CHAPTER TEN

NEITHER Michael nor Melanie persuaded her to stay in London, and both of them tried. But Juliet knew she was doing the right thing, knew that it was in Devon she had lost her identity, and that it was there that she would find it again—if it could be found.

Her mother gave a surprised 'Of course, dear' when Juliet asked if she might continue to stay at the cottage.

Her mother and Aunt Josephine had returned tanned and fit from Africa, the safari apparently having been a success with both of them, although the guide hadn't turned out to be the success her mother had thought he would be.

'He was married,' she explained dismissively.

Juliet only just stopped herself from asking what difference that made. It wasn't going to be easy to lose this bitterness towards her mother, but she knew she had to, if she was to be a complete person, if she was to be the type of woman Jake wanted. And she did want to be that woman.

Over the weeks she could see a subtle difference in her relationship with her mother. At first it had been difficult, their conversations strained, their friendship forced, but as the weeks passed it became easier, and they even started to joke together.

Juliet's work was going marvellously; Emily had married her doctor, causing a sensation by divorcing him when she found out about his affair with her mother, Edward was suddenly an enemy, and Charles her favourite now as they forced Edward out of his inheritance. Juliet knew exactly where the book was going to end, had mapped out a life of campaigning for women's rights for the embittered Emily, leaving the two half-brothers taking wives and having children of their own, children who would dominate the last book in the trilogy, *Mason's Ruin*, a book barely formed in Juliet's mind.

'I never realised how hard you had to work,' her mother remarked one day as she came to the end of an afternoon's writing, and the two of them were sitting out in the garden together as autumn began to turn the colours from green to gold.

Three months she had been here now, three months when she had only been up to London twice, both times to discuss the progress of the book with Michael, making fleeting visits to Melanie at the same time.

And it had been three months of discovering her mother, of coming to know the sad, often lonely woman behind the gaiety she showed the world. She was finally getting to know her mother—and she was liking what she found.

Juliet put her notebook down. 'Mummy . . .' She had unconsciously stopped using the stilted 'Mother' weeks ago.

'Yes, dear?' Her mother gave a clear, untroubled smile.

She licked her lips. 'I—I'm ready for that talk now.'

'You are?' Her mother didn't even pretend not to know what she meant.

'Yes,' she nodded. 'That is, if you want to talk to me. I—I wasn't very—receptive last time.'

Her mother looked at her searchingly. 'You've changed this last few months, Juliet. It wouldn't have anything to do with the "husband" you acquired while I was away, would it?'

Colour flooded her cheeks. 'Who——? Mrs Wiggins!' she sighed.

'It was Jake, wasn't it?' her mother asked gently.

'Yes,' she nodded, looking anywhere but at her mother.

'What do you want to know?' Estelle briskly changed the subject.

Juliet blinked dazedly. 'Don't you want to know about Jake being here?'

'No.'

'No?'

'Unless you want to tell me?'

She shrugged. 'It didn't work out.'

'But he did say something to you to give me a chance to have my daughter back.'

'Oh, Mummy!' Juliet looked at her with tear-filled eyes.

Her mother was equally affected. 'It might not have worked out between the two of you, but I'll always be grateful to him for giving you back to me.'

'So will I,' Juliet choked.

'Now, you want to know about your father and me,' her mother said with a sigh.

'If—if you want to tell me.'

'Even if your father doesn't come out the knight in armour you thought he was?' Estelle prompted anxiously.

'Even then,' Juliet nodded.

'Very well.' Her mother gave another deep sigh. 'I was eighteen when I met and fell in love with your father—he was almost thirty, very serious-natured. As you can imagine, I was a bit juvenile compared to him, but we fell in love anyway. For a year we were very happy together, and then—and then——'

'You became pregnant,' Juliet finished softly.

'Yes. Your father was delighted. And so was I, don't ever doubt that. It's just that that was the time the trouble started between us. You know I couldn't have any more children?'

'Yes,' she confirmed huskily, seeing how much pain

the memories still caused her mother.

'I don't want you to misunderstand your father, he was a good man, and kind to me, always. But some men just can't accept that.'

'Accept what?' Juliet frowned.

'To your father I was no longer a complete woman——'

'That's ridiculous!'

'Not to your father. I was twenty years old and my husband no longer wanted me, physically.'

'He—You——' Juliet was very pale, unable to believe what her mother was telling her. 'Are you saying that you and Daddy never—never made love after I was born?'

'Yes,' her mother nodded. 'Oh, I couldn't really blame him——'

'Well, I could!' Juliet said indignantly. 'It—It's inhuman! You must have suffered enough, without the added rejection from your husband.'

'It takes a very special man to understand how a woman feels at a time like that, your father just wasn't one of those men. But we stayed together, married and yet not married, with you our only source of interest. At times I couldn't stand not having your father's love, the loneliness, and so I would go away.'

'Did you—were there other men?'

Her mother shook her head. 'Never. I still cared for your father, no matter how he felt about me. And we had you.' Her face softened. 'You were the one thing that kept me sane. But as you got older it became apparent that the strained relationship between your father and me was affecting you, that you sensed it.'

'Which is why you sent me away to school.'

'Yes,' her mother smiled gently. 'Every time you had to go back there it broke my heart. But I didn't want you hurt by your parents' marriage. While no one else was involved I could stand the situation. Then—then——'

'Then Daddy had an affair,' Juliet realised dully.

'It wasn't an affair exactly, as far as I know it only
happened the once, and then it was just a question of
mutual need. I can see that now, two lonely people
turning to each other for comfort, but at the time it just
pushed more of a wedge between your father and me.
And I couldn't bear the thought of Josephine staying
here any longer.'

Juliet frowned her puzzlement. 'Aunt Josephine? But
what——'

'You still haven't realised, have you?' Her mother
gave a sad smile.

'Realised what?'

'That Josephine was the woman your father made
love to.'

'No!' she gasped, paling even more.

'Yes. Oh, it was a mistake on their part, they both
knew that. Josephine went to live in London after that,
and I—I just went abroad more. Your father lost himself
in his books once more.'

It explained so much—the estrangement between the
two sisters that had continued for years, the way her
Aunt Josephine had told her not to judge her mother
too harshly.

'Oh, Mummy, how did you stand it?' she cried.

Estelle shrugged. 'I had you. And although you may
not believe this, I still loved your father.'

Juliet shook her head. 'I don't see how you could.'

'Well, I did. I couldn't blame him for the way he
felt, and what happened between him and Josephine
was partly my own fault. I was away such a lot, I left
them alone here all the time, what happened was in-
evitable. Josephine was so full of shame, and your
father just seemed to retreat into himself. And through
it all it became obvious that you were starting to despise
me.'

'Oh, Mummy!'

'I know, darling,' Estelle squeezed her hand. 'But you loved your father, so if anything good had come out of the marriage it was that. When he died I thought perhaps we would finally grow closer together, but instead you left to live in London.' She chewed on her lower lip. 'Jim and Robert may be harder to explain.'

'No,' Juliet shook her head. 'They were people who cared for you, made you feel a woman, and after eighteen years of indifference you deserved that. I'm only sorry they didn't work out.'

Her mother gave a shaky smile. 'Thank you.'

'Maybe one day——'

'No more husbands, Juliet,' Estelle laughed. 'I think I'll just settle for grandchildren.'

'Mummy——'

'Jake cares for you,' she said gently. 'I could see that much from the short time I saw you together. And you love him, don't you?'

'Yes.'

'Does he want children?'

'Oh yes!' Juliet remembered their first conversation.

'Then would four be asking too much?'

'Mummy!'

'Well, would it?' Estelle teased.

Juliet blushed. 'I have no idea whether Jake cares for me that deeply.'

'But if he does?'

'Then you can have half a dozen—a dozen grandchildren,' she gave a happy laugh.

'Juliet,' her mother was serious now, 'I don't want what I've told you to affect your friendship with Josephine.'

'It won't,' Juliet said with certainty. 'I think I'm adult enough now to understand. Six months ago I wouldn't have been,' she added ruefully.

Her mother smiled. 'Six months ago I don't think I would have told you—not all of it.'

Three months later Juliet was ready to return to London. The book was completed and sent to Michael two months earlier than the deadline, all hitches ironed out, just ready to go into print.

Her relationship with her mother couldn't have been better, and she knew that this six months together had made them closer than a lot of mothers and daughters ever were. Her mother had not gone away in all of that time, and the bond between them had grown stronger and stronger.

Her Aunt Josephine had come to stay for a couple of weeks, and not once, by word or deed, did she show she knew anything about the past. She knew her aunt was pleased by the closeness between mother and daughter, perhaps some of her own guilt erased.

Juliet maybe wouldn't have returned to London even then if Michael hadn't telephoned the evening before to say Melanie had given him a beautiful little girl.

'You didn't exaggerate,' Juliet told Michael as she bent over the tiny crib. 'She really is lovely.'

'At least I don't have to suffer the name Josiah,' the proud father grimaced.

'We could have a boy next time,' Melanie warned.

'Next time?' He looked startled.

'Oh yes,' Melanie told him teasingly. 'I've never believed in only children.'

'Now she tells me!' he groaned.

'Go on,' Juliet laughed. 'You're loving it all.'

'Yes,' he smiled. 'But I have to leave now,' he told his wife regretfully. 'I have to see someone this afternoon.'

'Of course you do, darling,' Melanie said understandingly. 'I have to feed Angel, anyway.'

'Why Angel?' Juliet asked.

'Because she looks like one,' Melanie grinned.

'I agree,' she laughed. 'Michael, I have to talk to you some time,' she added seriously.

'Now?'

'Not if you're in a hurry,' she shook her head.

He glanced at his wrist-watch. 'I can spare you a couple of minutes.'

'Would you mind?' Juliet asked Melanie. 'It isn't private or anything.'

'No, go ahead,' her friend invited cheerfully, starting to feed Angel.

Juliet drew in a deep breath. 'I'd like for you to arrange for Caroline Miles to go on Jake's show,' she told Michael calmly.

His eyes widened. 'You would?'

She nodded. 'Can you do it?'

'Without question.'

'Then—will you?' she looked at him anxiously.

'You know Jake always meets the authors before they go on the show,' Michael warned.

'I'm counting on it,' she nodded.

'Juliet, you aren't going to do anything stupid?'

'Michael,' his wife cut in firmly, her gaze fixed on Juliet's face, 'just do it.'

'But——'

'Michael,' she repeated, 'doing something stupid is the last thing Juliet has on her mind.'

'Okay,' he shrugged. 'I'll get in touch with Jake today, and I'll call you later. At the flat, right?'

'Right,' she confirmed.

'I was right, wasn't I?' Melanie said once Michael had left. 'Doing something stupid isn't what you have in mind, is it?'

She pulled a face. 'Depends how you look at it. I— Have you seen Jake at all lately?'

'We've had him to dinner about three times in the last six months, if that's what you mean.'

'And does he—does he have someone—special in his life at the moment?' Juliet dreaded the answer, knowing that Jake was too attractive to be alone all this time.

Besides, they had said 'goodbye', not 'see you'.

'Well, he's never brought anyone with him, if that's what you mean,' her friend told her. 'And he's never taken anyone home either. And he always asks how you are.'

'He does?' Juliet asked eagerly.

'Mm. I told him you were in Devon with your mother, and he—he seemed pleased.'

'Yes,' Juliet smiled.

'He's the one, isn't he?' Melanie probed gently.

'Yes,' she didn't attempt to prevaricate. 'It's seven months since I first met him, and six months without him, and I still love him.'

'And Ben and Stephen?'

Juliet smiled. 'Ben thinks he's at last met the girl who will love him for himself—her father is richer than he is! And Stephen is concentrating on Blake Engineering. His father has been told to take it easy, so Stephen is enjoying the extra responsibility.'

Melanie squeezed her hand. 'I hope it all works out for you.'

Michael telephoned her that evening. 'Monday night for dinner, okay?' he asked without preamble.

'Where?' She was just as direct.

'Ricardo's. It's——'

'I know where it is,' she assured him. It was the restaurant Jake had taken her to on their first date. 'What time?'

'Eight o'clock. But, Juliet——'

'Thanks, Michael,' she interrupted firmly. 'I'll let you know how things go.'

The weekend passed very slowly; so much depended on this meeting with Jake that she hardly dared think about it.

But suddenly it was eight o'clock on Monday, and her heart was leaping into her throat as she stepped out of the taxi at Ricardo's. She looked her best, she knew she did, her black dress sophisticated and yet simple in design, emphasising the perfection of her body. Her hair was newly washed and gleaming, her light make-up highlighting the sherry-coloured eyes Jake liked so much.

Jake was sitting at the same table they had occupied before, standing up as the waiter escorted her to the table, not showing even by a flicker of emotion that he was surprised or shocked to see her.

Juliet sat down, watching as Jake did the same, looking dark and distinguished in his black evening suit. He looked just the same, dark and attractive, and yet there was a difference, a harshness that hadn't been there before, a cynical twist to his well-shaped mouth.

'What would you like to drink, Miss Miles?' he drawled suddenly. 'Ah yes, whisky and ginger, if I remember correctly.'

'Jake——'

He signalled the waiter, requesting the drink. 'What would you like to eat?' he asked with that cold politeness. 'I believe the duck is very good.'

This wasn't going at all as she wanted it to. Jake was like a stranger, and she had no idea how to get past the barrier he had erected between them. 'Michael told you,' she sighed.

'Told me what?' he looked at her with calm blue eyes.

'That I'm Caroline Miles.'

'No,' he shook his head, 'you told me that.'

'I didn't!' she gasped.

'But you did.'

'How?'

'You gave me a manuscript to read.' He shrugged. 'I told you that everyone has their own style of writing. You might as well have put your signature on that manuscript—or rather Caroline Miles'.'

'You knew even then?' Her face mirrored her dismay.

'Yes.'

'Then why didn't you say something?'

Jake looked thoughtful. 'At first I was annoyed, angry. I figured you were taking me for a fool because of the remarks I'd made about *Mason's Heritage*.' He saw her colour guiltily. 'Yes, I thought I was right. You planned to wait until a vulnerable moment and then tell me who you were. But by the time I'd read that manuscript there'd already been too many—vulnerable moments. And you hadn't done a damned thing except kiss and touch me back.'

'I changed my mind,' she admitted.

He nodded. 'I realised that. I was already too involved with you to dare to probe why.'

'Involved . . .?'

'Attracted,' he amended abruptly. 'At the time I hadn't realised what a confused child you really were, the bitterness inside you. When Michael telephoned on Friday and told me Caroline Miles was willing to do the interview I knew you'd decided to pay me back after all. Well, it isn't necessary now. I'd just like to say one thing before I leave.'

'Leave?' she echoed dazedly.

'Yes. The joke's over. It wasn't very funny to start with.'

'I know that,' she sighed.

'Then why the hell——? Never mind,' Jake took a controlling breath. 'I've read *Mason's Fortune*, Juliet. Michael lent me a pre-publication copy. It's good. It's human, loving, tragic, even funny on occasion. It's a book about life—real life, not a life of a bitter enclosed woman. You're capable of loving now, Juliet,' he said emotionlessly.

'Yes,' she confirmed huskily. 'I—My mother—I was so wrong about her. We—we're friends now.'

'I'm glad. Now shall we end this?' He stood up. 'You stay and have a meal if you want one, I'm really not hungry.'

'Jake——'

'Goodbye, Miss Miles.' He strode off.

Goodbye, Miss Miles, goodbye, Miss Miles. The words kept going round and round in her mind. Goodbye, he had said. But she didn't want it to be goodbye! She wouldn't *let* it be goodbye.

Jake had long gone by the time she had picked up her bag and explained to the confused waiter that neither Jake nor herself would be staying to eat. And then she had trouble getting a taxi, making it almost an hour after they had parted that she arrived outside Jake's door, ringing the bell before she changed her mind, fearing rejection again.

Jake had changed since he got home, and was now wearing the casual shirt and denims she liked him in best, his eyes widening as he saw her.

'Juliet . . .?'

'I love you, Jake,' she told him clearly. 'I know what love is, how to love—you said yourself I knew that now, and I know I love you.'

He pulled her roughly into his arms. 'I thought you'd never get here,' he murmured shakily into her hair.

'Get here?' she repeated dazedly. 'But I—I don't understand. How did you know I was coming here?'

'I didn't—not definitely.' He pulled her inside his flat and closed the door, turning to cup her face in his hands, bending to kiss her gently, almost reverently, on the lips. 'I love you, Juliet,' he told her huskily. 'This past six months have seemed like six years.'

'To me too.' She returned his fevered kisses unreservedly. 'But what did you mean, you were expecting me but then again you weren't?'

He put his arm about her shoulders, taking her over to the sofa to sit down beside her. 'The woman I met tonight at the restaurant was Caroline Miles. I wanted Juliet Chase to come to me, the woman I knew was my perfect partner in life. I think I knew that from the moment we first met.'

'Jake, will you marry me?'

'Will I what?' he gave an outraged laugh.

'Will you marry me—not Juliet or Caroline, but me?'

'I'd marry you if you were an Agnes or a Gertrude!' He kissed her until both their heads spun.

'Even if you have to have a dozen children?' she teased happily.

'A dozen?' he looked astounded.

Juliet nodded. 'I told my mother we would if you would marry me.'

Jake grinned. 'I wouldn't want to disappoint your mother.'

'Or me?'

'Certainly not you,' he said throatily.

'I love you so much, Jake,' she told him, her eyes glowing.

'I should hope so, when you've just asked me to marry you!'

'Are you—annoyed about my being Caroline Miles?' she asked apprehensively.

'Of course not. I was disappointed that you didn't tell me before, I tried to give you the opportunity to several times, especially when I told you I was going to try and get Caroline Miles on my show, but it didn't work.'

'I was too shocked to tell you anything,' she said ruefully. 'I saw your interview with Broderick McCormick, by the way. It was really good. It made the top five ratings, didn't it?'

'Mm,' Jake nodded. 'But don't we have better things to do than talk about McCormick?'

She gave him a coy look beneath lowered lashes. 'Are you asking me to spend the night with you?' she asked with pretended shock.

'Will you?'

Juliet moved out of his arms, standing up to open her handbag, sorting through its contents.

'What are you doing?' Jake frowned.

'I'm looking for—ah, found it.' She put her handbag down, turning to leave the room.

Jake stood up. 'Where are you going?'

'To put my toothbrush in the bathroom.' She held it up, and ducked out of the room, laughing happily at the look of incredulity on Jake's face.

'Juliet——!' He ran after her, catching up with her outside his bedroom, capturing her in his arms to curve her body against his. 'Your toothbrush can wait until later,' he growled. 'But after six months, *I* can't!'

TASTY CORNISH PASTY

When Juliet and Jake fly to Cornwall, Jake samples his
first real Cornish pasty, a delicious individual meat pie
for which Cornwall is famous. We thought you might
enjoy making this tasty treat for yourself.

Pasty pastry

    2 cups all-purpose flour
    ½ cup butter
    2 tbsp. lard
    1 egg yolk
    3 tbsp. cold water
    1 egg white, lightly beaten

Sift flour into a large mixing bowl. Cut butter and lard
into small pieces and mix into flour until well coated.
Using your fingers, knead the pieces of fat into the flour
until the mixture has the texture of breadcrumbs. Beat
egg yolk and water together, add to flour mixture and
blend. Gently knead on a floured board until dough is
smooth. Return dough to bowl, cover and cool in
refrigerator for 20 minutes.

Pasty filling

    1 lb. chuck steak, cut into ½-inch cubes
    1 tbsp. oil
    1 large onion, chopped
    1 cup carrot, diced
    1 tsp. salt
    pepper to taste

In a large skillet, brown meat in oil. Add onion and
sauté. Remove from heat and mix in carrot, salt and
pepper. Preheat oven to 400°F. (205°C.). Roll out chilled
dough to ¼-inch thickness. Cut into four circles about 5
inches in diameter. Divide meat mixture into four and
place in middle of pastry circles. Fold each pastry circle
around the meat mixture to make a half-moon shape,
then pinch edges together to seal mixture in. Glaze with
egg white and bake for 30 minutes.

Legacy of PASSION

BY CATHERINE KAY

A love story begun long ago comes full circle...

Venice, 1819: Contessa Allegra di Rienzi, young, innocent, unhappily married. She gave her love to Lord Byron—scandalous, irresistible English poet. Their brief, tempestuous affair left her with a shattered heart, a few poignant mementos—and a daughter he never knew about.

Boston, today: Allegra Brent, modern, independent, restless. She learned the secret of her great-great-great-grandmother and journeyed to Venice to find the di Rienzi heirs. There she met the handsome, cynical, blood-stirring Conte Renaldo di Rienzi, and like her ancestor before her, recklessly, hopelessly lost her heart.

What the press says about Harlequin romance fiction...

"When it comes to romantic novels...
Harlequin is the indisputable king."
—*New York Times*

" 'Harlequin [is]... the best and the biggest.' "
—*Associated Press* (quoting Janet Dailey's husband, Bill)

"The most popular reading matter of
American women today."
—*Detroit News*

"... exciting escapism, easy reading, interesting
characters and, always, a happy ending....
They are hard to put down."
—*Transcript-Telegram*, Holyoke (Mass.)

"... a work of art."
—*Globe & Mail*, Toronto

Harlequin Presents...

Take these 4 best-selling novels FREE

Yes! Four sophisticated,
contemporary love stories
by four world-famous
authors of romance
FREE, as your
introduction to the Harlequin Presents
subscription plan. Thrill to **Anne Mather**'s
passionate story BORN OUT OF LOVE, set
in the Caribbean.... Travel to darkest Africa
in **Violet Winspear**'s TIME OF THE TEMPTRESS....Let
Charlotte Lamb take you to the fascinating world of London's
Fleet Street in MAN'S WORLD....Discover beautiful Greece in
Sally Wentworth's moving romance SAY HELLO TO YESTERDAY.

Join the millions of avid Harlequin readers all over the
world who delight in the magic of a really exciting novel.
EIGHT great NEW titles published EACH MONTH!
Each month you will get to know exciting, interesting,
true-to-life people .... You'll be swept to distant lands you've
dreamed of visiting .... Intrigue, adventure, romance, and
the destiny of many lives will thrill you through each
Harlequin Presents novel.

*The very finest
in romance fiction*

Get all the latest books before they're sold out!

As a Harlequin subscriber you actually receive your
personal copies of the latest Presents novels immediately
after they come off the press, so you're sure of getting all
8 each month.

Cancel your subscription whenever you wish!

You don't have to buy any minimum number of books.
Whenever you decide to stop your subscription just let us
know and we'll cancel all further shipments.

Your FREE gift includes

Anne Mather—Born out of Love
Violet Winspear—Time of the Temptress
Charlotte Lamb—Man's World
Sally Wentworth—Say Hello to Yesterday